CHRONICLES OF ESHA 3

DESTINY
OF THE
SWORD

TABITHA DAY

ISBN 978-0473-73062-8 (ePub)

ISBN 978-0473-73061-1 (Paperback)

ISBN 978-0473-73063-5 (Kindle)

Cover designed by GetCovers

Powered by Atticus

For those who have found that everything is up to them.

THE STORY SO FAR

BETRAYAL OF THE SWORD, CHRONICLES OF ESHA 2

The Adjudicator has forced Ember back to the Kingdom of Swords to return the pendant containing the Blade. Unfortunately, the Blade has bonded with Ember, and Cole and Ashe must fight for it again.

A chance meeting with a mage from the Kingdom of Stones has revealed a twist to Ember's past—she has fae blood, and the ruler of the Stones is convinced she belongs to them.

In the final contest, Cole is apparently victorious, and Ashe condemned to be the Blade ... but it is a ruse. Serafina, Cole's sister and Ashe's first love, has returned from the dead and now holds the kingdom while the Adjudicator pulls her strings.

With the peace of Esha at risk, Ember decides not to return to Earth. She's going to stay and fight for the one she loves ...

Chapter 1

Ember crouched behind the line of shrubs, watching the fae lope across the clearing, his spear held lightly in one hand. He looked left and right, scanning the ground for footprints, broken foliage, disturbed leaves, any sign she'd passed by. She tried to keep her breathing slow and silent, covering her mouth and nose with her fleece muffler for fear a telltale wisp of breath would give her away. The foliage was sparse, the bare twigs stark against the snow, but she'd managed to get the hang of camouflage in the past few weeks. Her skin and clothing were almost perfectly matched to her environment, and as she shifted to get a better grip on her own spear, the muted colours of snow, rocks, branches and grey green grass rippled across her body. She was a chameleon, a pane of glass, invisible to the eye —

"I can see you, Ember," he said, and his voice held a hint of laughter.

She scowled, but didn't reply. More than once, he'd tricked her into showing herself.

"You're behind the bushes."

There was a blur of movement and quicker than thought, his spear hurtled toward her. She fell back into the snow, and it hissed over her head. Her breath gusted in an outraged cry, her camouflage disappearing and leaving her perfectly visible in a grey suede outfit of pants and tunic, a white hood on her head. The fae jogged over to her, wrenching his spear out of the bushes where it had caught fast in the branches, and whirled it, tossing it lightly from hand to hand.

Indignant, she yanked her muffler down. "How?"

"You forgot your feet."

She glanced down at the sturdy boots which had resisted her fae power of disguise and burst out laughing. "That must have looked ridiculous."

He held out a hand and pulled her to her feet, bringing her in for a warm embrace. She held him close for just a moment, enjoying the feel of his strong arms around her, and then pulled away.

His evident disappointment was quickly concealed with a practised courtier's smile. "It's getting chilly. Do you want to go in yet?"

"Oh, Kalin. You always want to finish training before I do."

"I've never seen anyone such a glutton for punching, hiding, and shooting. The ladies of the court are quite scandalised."

"Apoli asked if she could come shooting the next time I was out," Ember defended herself. "I think I may have started a trend."

Kalin gave a wry laugh. "*I* think her target is the master of bows. I'd better warn him."

"Apoli would never forgive you."

"Just a quick session, then. I do not wish to tire you."

She tucked her hand into the crook of his arm, and the two headed back across the snow-covered lawns toward the palace. It was nearly the end of winter in the Kingdom of Stones—although spring was just a gentle thaw before autumn came and winter descended again—and the weather was still inclement enough that Kalin insisted they practise archery in the palace training arenas rather than in the gardens. The training arenas were enclosed by walls and roof, redolent of the smell of sawdust scattered on the dirt floors—best for soaking up accidental spills of blood—and the warmer climate was kinder to the wooden practise bows than the temperatures of outdoors.

Their companionable silence was broken by the heavy percussion of wind buffeted by massive wings. Both instinctively looked skyward and broke into a run.

"Has she seen us?" Ember panted as they hit the snow-covered trail at speed, feet thumping a staccato beat along the slippery path edged with snowdaisies, the perpetually blooming flower of the kingdom.

"Of course she's seen us," Kalin said grimly. In response, there came a loud screech that made both wince. The beating of wings paused, a dreadful silence of anticipation filling the air.

"She's diving," Ember cried, and then the mighty wings snapped out with a ferocious *smack*, which was shortly followed by a thud that shook the earth, a blizzard of snow scattering from the snowy branches all around them.

Ember drew to a halt, panting, as Diamond confronted them. If she had been human, she would have her hands on her hips, her foot tapping an impatient tattoo. But she was pure dragon, and her aggrieved temper was expressed by narrowed chartreuse eyes, a ripple of muscles under dull green scales, a show of gleaming fangs, and a warning coil of black smoke from her nostrils.

"I'm sorry," Ember said. "I wasn't allowed to go out today."

She approached the dragon, inhaling the smell of her with pleasure, an adventurous scent of smouldering wet leaves and burning charcoal, and then leaned against her, stroking Diamond's gleaming chest scales with a leather gloved hand. The dragon gave a funny mewling sound of pleasure, showing her to be the youngster she still was, only newly released from her leash, and still learning the ways of survival in the mountains and as a member of the palace fleet.

Kalin hovered back on the path. Diamond tolerated him, but she adored Ember and was always a little jealous of anyone else who came too close.

"Sten and Ruby and some of their dragon-riders went on a fact-finding mission," she continued. "I wasn't invited."

The Stones always maintained that the dragons understood them perfectly well, and never treated them like dogs or beasts of burden. The official dragon-riders of the palace fleet had such a bond with their mounts that they could communicate with them by thought alone—*firespeech*—although this wasn't a gift that she and Diamond shared.

Diamond nudged Ember with her great head as if urging Ember to continue, and she hastily continued, "It appears the Sword has not been treating her people well."

This was a massive understatement. From the reports filtering through to the Kingdom of Stones, it seemed Serafina had rapidly and happily assumed the role of benevolent dictator—without the benevolent bit. Several fae in prominent positions had either disappeared or had been shipped out to villages on the kingdom's outskirts, ostensibly for their health, but more likely to inhibit their interference with the running of the kingdom. With the exodus of the centaurs, the healing clinics and schools were closed, and the common fae were suffering. And worst of all, the Adjudicator was still in residence, showing that he was indeed pulling Serafina's strings, even though she professed to be the independent ruler—with Ashe, of course, confined in the pendant around her throat.

Ember's heart constricted at the thought of Ashe. The last words he had spoken to her were so full of sadness, his eyes haunted. *"I was always destined to be the Blade,"* he had said, and yet, she knew that wasn't true. He should have ruled the Kingdom of Swords. Not his dead ex-lover, and not his unhinged cousin. Cole hadn't been seen in months, and most assumed he was dead. It was an anticlimactic end to his short and brutal time as heir, and Ember held not a shred of regret at his demise.

Diamond let out a soft purr, as if she could indeed read Ember's thoughts and was trying to comfort her, and Ember smiled. "Good girl. I have to go. We're going to practise archery now."

Diamond turned to Kalin and gave a brisk snort, and Kalin gave a mock salute back. The dragon turned and lumbered forward a few clumsy steps before launching herself into the sky, barely clearing the trees before disappearing into the clouds.

"I thought she would have singed you at least."

Ember laughed. "She hasn't done that in weeks."

Being allowed to help with Diamond's training had been a singular honour, one which she knew Sten had pushed for over Ruby's protestations. It had taken weeks of feeding and grooming and establishing trust before she was allowed to sit on Diamond's back, much less been allowed to fly with her, and it was a privilege she wasn't about to squander. The only reason Ruby had relented at all was the affectionate bond that had quickly developed between the young dragon and Ember, even if actual telepathy was beyond them both.

Kalin reached for her hand and gently kissed her knuckles. "It's truly wonderful how well you've fitted into our little kingdom—"

"Little!" Ember scoffed, for the Kingdom of Stones' territory was huge, a vast stretch of mountains, frozen lakes, and forests of ice tucked into the dark valleys that saw the sun for barely a month out of every thirteen.

"—and I hope you're proud of how far you've come. Even Danida is mildly impressed."

Which was high praise considering Danida, her tutor of spells and enchantments, had often raged about her 'ignorant human mind' and her 'stubborn inability to reach the competency of a small child'.

"There's still a lot I can't do," she said, counting off on her fingers. "I can't make light properly, I can't do glamours without Alena's brush, and apparently I can't even camouflage my feet."

Kalin stopped her protests with a light kiss, a mere feather-soft brush across her lips.

She pulled away. "I suppose I should be thankful for what I *can* do."

If he had noticed that she had stepped away to avoid a closer embrace, he didn't make comment on it. Kalin was a higher member of the court, with more than his fair share of admirers. He was striking—even for a fae—strong, fearless and intelligent, and she knew he had convinced himself it was only a matter of time before they were together, properly. She hadn't disabused him of the notion, for she found his company comfortable, and he was fun to train with, but she hadn't encouraged him either. How could she, with the memory of dark eyes searing her, the last thing she ever saw in her mind's eye before she fell asleep, and that familiar sultry scent drifting through the air while she was waking, although it had always disappeared by the time she was fully awake.

"You're good with barriers, and you can see through glamours, even if you can't cast them well. The dragons accept you, and your shooting is ..." Kalin gave a polite cough. "Getting better."

She dug an elbow into his ribs. "Well, that's why we're practising!"

He laughed, and she was relieved they were once again back in easy territory as friends.

By the time they reached the arena, servants were waiting with warming drinks to chase the last vestiges of outdoor chill away, and baskets of arrows with several choices of bow. The servant handed a bow to Ember, which was just her size and relatively easy to draw, but Kalin swapped it for a heavier one, telling her she had to work on her strength. His own bow was huge, and she had neither the muscle nor the technique to even pull the bowstring back.

He waited for her to draw, and then adjusted her elbows and stance before she let the arrow fly. It found the edge of the target, and she gave a whoop of delight. It had taken her weeks of training to get to this point, and she had often despaired of doing it at all. There was a *thunk*, and an arrow quivered dead centre, Kalin looking suitably modest and shrugging carelessly.

"I think there was perhaps a slight breeze when you shot."

"Kalin," she said. "We're indoors."

They shared a chuckle at the familiar, well-worn joke, and when the servant handed her another arrow, she shot again and again and again. She could have happily stayed there all evening, but presently the door behind them opened to admit one of the King's servants, bowing low with a message. "The One requests the presence of Ember in the throne room."

Ember and Kalin exchanged a startled glance. If Sten wanted to talk with her, he usually just appeared, informally, as one friend to another. The command for an audience was unusual. "Do you know why?"

The servant bowed again. "Apparently, the fair heir of the Swords has been seen in the Kingdom of Seeds."

Ember felt an icy hand reach into her gut and squeeze.

Cole.

CHAPTER 2

S ten, the One, and Ruby, the Two, sat on their respective thrones, ten warrior guards arrayed behind them, advisors and several courtiers gathered in front of the dais. Ember was accustomed to being treated as an honoured guest, and the fae here were much more welcoming and friendly than those of the Swords had been. Despite that, the array of powerful fae in the room brought a nervous dampness to her palms, and she approached their majesties with a certain amount of deference in her step, bowing low when she reached them.

"Ember, darling. I understand we interrupted your archery practise," said Ruby. "We apologise for that."

Ember was quick to shake her head and demur, as all the fae turned to stare. "That's fine, honestly."

She could feel heat crawling up her cheeks. Of late, she'd thought Ruby annoyed with her presence in the kingdom. Certainly, she was as pleasant as ever, but more than once she'd chosen to single her out in a room full of fae, even though she was well aware Ember disliked being the centre of attention. Ember was the only human in a world of fae, always the subject of sidelong glances and gossip, and it grew wearying. Sten must have been aware of this too, for he shot Ruby an irritated glance, to which she returned a bland smile.

They waited in silence for a few more minutes, and then two more fae arrived, breathless with hurrying. Scholars, both of them, the ink-spotted hands and chalk-dusted robes giving them away.

Sten spread his hands expansively and said without preamble, "Cole has been seen in the Kingdom of Seeds. The Swords are also calling in their banners from the countryside—ostensibly to welcome the new ruler. However, an army of considerable size amassing together should never be ignored."

Although she'd already heard the news of Cole, Sten's words still gave Ember an unpleasant jolt. If Cole was in the Seeds' territory, it was for one reason only: to make mischief.

"We have long considered sending a delegation to the Sands to prevent them from joining the Seeds in this ... folly."

"We can only ask," Ruby reprimanded gently. She raised her voice and said, "The Kingdom of Stones does not condone meddling in another kingdom's affairs." Her gaze fell on Ember lightly before skating away. "Officially."

"Officially," agreed Sten. "But we must do what we can for the sake of peace in Esha. The Seeds can only make war on the Free Grasslands with the Swords' assistance, and if the Sands are drawn in as well—"

He paused, and the echo of his words seemed to fill the throne room. "The Swords cannot be allowed to run roughshod over the rest of us. Curtailing their power must be our highest priority."

Ruby nodded. "You will all join the delegation in the company of the One and Two to the Kingdom of Sands."

None of the fae moved, or showed any sign of reaction at all, neither pleasure at being chosen nor dismay at leaving the kingdom—such was their training to remain stoic in front of their superiors—but Ember rocked back on her heels as if she'd been struck. Leave the safety of the Stones? She'd lived there for months now, regarded it as home. The Adjudicator and the Swords thought she'd returned to Earth, that her interference in the crowning of the Sword was over and done with. If they suspected she was alive and here in Esha, if they knew she was training to fight and learning how to bring forth the magic hidden within her, to discover what it meant to be part-fae, would they come after her?

"Ember," said Sten, as if guessing the direction of her thoughts, "We're aware of the dangers of sending you along, but we feel that your unique perspective as a ... er ... foreigner might help with the negotiations. Your insights and such. We'll disguise you as fae. Don't worry. They won't know."

Ember nodded, somewhat mollified, and as the discussion soon turned to practicalities, her spirits rose. The Kingdom of Sands! She'd heard many tales about the magnificent bazaars, the hidden oasis gardens, and the royal palace which shifted with the sandstorms and was renowned for being the most refined, the most beautiful, in all of Esha. Ember found this hard to believe; she loved the Stones' palace, with its arching ceilings, marble floors, carved wall panels and the clear light that streamed through the open window views of snow-capped mountains. It was difficult to imagine anything more majestic. And then her thoughts turned to the practicalities of travel and her heart sank. Walking through the column portals would have been the easiest choice; the delegates only numbered around twenty. It would be a quick, easy trip through the portal directly into the Sand's territory. But Ember had always found the columns a traumatic experience, and the thought of vomiting on arrival during an official court visit made her stomach churn in anticipatory chagrin. But no, it appeared they had a different idea.

"We'll take the dragons," Sten announced.

"A show of strength will show the Sands who they're dealing with," Ruby said. "Let's remind them whose side they should be on."

The dragons' magic and strength were at their peak in the mountains and Ember wondered if the heat of the desert and its distance from their home would sap the dragons' strength, but perhaps their presence was all that was needed to project an image of force, a guise to match her own as a full fae. Her spirits rose. Flying a dragon across the country to visit the most beautiful palace in Esha? If it wasn't such a serious matter, it would be the trip of a lifetime.

The One's first advisor announced the meeting was over, and the delegation bowed before leaving the room. But Ember lingered, hoping to make a request without the entire court looking on.

Eventually Sten noticed her and said, "Did you want something?"

"Yes, Your Majesty. I wondered if I might take Diamond?"

Sten frowned. "She's a little too young and flighty, I think. We thought you might fly with the scholars on Garantis."

Ember's face fell. Taking Diamond would have been the ultimate cherry on top. Ruby, however, gave an indulgent wave.

"If the dragon-master agrees, of course, you may."

Ember didn't stop to wonder at the change of heart, merely giving a breathless "Thank you," and making a hasty retreat before Sten could cut in and change Ruby's mind.

She tore up to her chambers as fast as she could, so she could inspect her wardrobe. What on earth was she going to wear to the desert?

CHAPTER 3

The palace didn't have a stable for their fleet of dragons, for they would have burned it down in five seconds flat before tearing each other apart. Once they were old enough to be unleashed, the dragons flew to the vast reaches of the mountainous landscape, laying claim to whichever cavern took their fancy, guided by whatever navigational system lay within them. They lived solitary lives, only coming together to breed and fight—and fights were rare, usually over territory. Ember had watched open-mouthed as two dragons mated in midair, a writhing, twisting column of gleaming scales and roaring fire that brought an unexpected blush to her cheeks and a wet warmth between her legs as she remembered how she and Ashe had once done more or less the same thing. Just once though, he'd said. She wished she'd been strong enough to tell him no, once would never be enough.

Ruby and Sten summoned the fleet by arcane means, but the delegation had to wait a few days for them to arrive. As Kalin often said, dragons were not dogs bred to obey. They were more like cats in their temperament—complying when they felt like it, and ignoring requests when they didn't.

But, over the coming days, they arrived with deafening screeches that rang around the grounds of the palace, before descending on the tabalor—a huge outdoor arena of stone inlaid with decorative drops of obsidian—to be harnessed and saddled for the outgoing flight. The largest would carry four or five fae, but Diamond, the smallest, would only carry Ember.

"I don't like it," Kalin said grimly, checking the straps and buckles for about the hundredth time. "She's untrained, she's too young, and you're not experienced enough to manage her."

Ember had been hearing comments from him like this for days now, and she was getting heartily sick of it. Diamond gave a smoky snort just as Ember said "pffft" and they glanced at each other in surprise. Ember laughed, rubbing Diamond's gleaming sides. "I'll be fine. Besides, if she doesn't listen to me, she'll listen to the others. They're bigger than her, and she knows they'll snap if she does anything wrong."

"You might get lost," Kalin growled, refusing to be mollified. "She's smaller than the rest. She might fall behind."

"I've seen a map. I know where the desert is. I'll just point her in the right direction."

"Yes, but—"

"Please stop fussing." Ember's tone was mild, but it held an edge of rebuke. She was no longer someone who could be bullied and controlled. The king and queen had selected her for this diplomatic mission. She'd trained with Diamond for months. The dragon-master had agreed the flight would be good for them. She wasn't going to screw it up.

Kalin took her hand, his eyes liquid with remorse. "I apologise. I just fear for your safety."

She gave him a brisk hug, a hug which was supposed to convey friendship and nothing more, but he took the opportunity to hold her close, and she suspected he was nuzzling her hair. She hastily stepped back. "I'll be fine. And I'll bring you back a souvenir. Something sandy."

A handler approached with Diamond's pack bags and the dragon settled on her haunches, flattening herself to the ground to give the handler easier access, and throwing Kalin a smug look which clearly said, "See? I can be good."

All across the tabalor, dragons were readied for flight, and the dragonsong ringing around the arena was both eerie and ear-splitting. Compared to the others, Diamond was tiny. Sten's dragon was massive, an older male called Lakin who was around three hundred years old, and he stood stoic and unmoving as servants climbed aboard, tightening straps and checking bundles. Ruby's dragon, Beni, was just a shade smaller, outfitted with bright crimson trappings as a vanity to Ruby and because, she said, Beni liked to look pretty. The Kings and Queens of the Stones always met their demise at the same time, and so keeping one safe at home in case of a flight mishap made little sense. Still, each had two servants, one before and one aft, to help protect and assist them on their journey.

The Stone mage appeared at the top of the sweeping staircase that led to the tabalor. He was dressed in his habitual grey robes, giving the impression he had materialised from the paving stones beneath his feet. He raised a hand, and an aura of calm descended over the area. The dragonsong quietened to a soft, mewling welcome, as the fae turned to watch him approach.

"Your Majesties!" He bowed to Sten and Ruby and then raised a hand to encompass the rest. "Travellers and adventurers!" The ringing tones sent an aura of anticipation and excitement around the arena, and Ember could feel her heart banging against her chest, the blood thrumming in her veins. "May you undertake this journey with open hearts, sound judgement and courageous action. The peace of Esha depends on you."

Sparkles of gold fell from the sky, descending on skin, scales, clothing and stone, a blessing cast by one of the most powerful mages in the country. It was an extraordinary sight to see everyone covered in gold, and when it melted away, the mage disappeared too. But the gift of peace and confidence he had given them remained, and Ember leapt up onto Diamond's back as though they were setting out for a fun day's ride, instead of a diplomatic mission fraught with danger. She strapped herself in and gave Kalin a wave.

"Don't worry," she called down to him. "All will be well."

He gave her a smile, but it was still taut, anxiety showing in his eyes. He retreated to the side of the arena with the others farewelling the party, and the delegation mounted. Ember slid her hands into the saddle's handholds. Dragons weren't bridled for obvious reasons—one burp and it would burst into flames—but there were two small handlebars rising from the saddle. The padded grips were in contact with the dragon's skin, and by pushing, pulling or pressing, Ember could signal her intentions, or even direct Diamond after a fashion—if Diamond decided it was in her best interests to be directed, of course. Still, the young dragon appeared in awe of the older, more experienced beasts, and she was on her best behaviour.

"Riders!" Sten cried, and Lakin reared up on its hind legs and roared, a roar which set Ember's teeth jangling in her head. The dragon took two mighty steps and launched into the air with a massive clap of thunder as the heavy wings snapped out and took the breeze. Ruby followed, and then the rest of the advisors and guards, until finally it was Diamond's turn.

It took Diamond four or five lumbering steps before she had enough power to launch herself over the parapet, and even then, Ember thought Diamond might scrape her belly on the stones, but they were over, catching the wind current and soaring into the sky.

A procession of dragons stretched out before her, and the day was calm and clear. Ember couldn't help a whoop of pure adrenaline and happiness, and Diamond gave an answering rumble from deep within her belly Ember could feel through her thighs and handholds, as if the beast was enjoying it as much as she was.

CHAPTER 4

T he fleet flew through the mountains, circling majestic peaks and skimming over icy lakes. They swooped low over a snowy forest, startling a flock of firebirds, who rose out of the pines squawking in terror, leaving trails of red sparks that Diamond flew through almost contemptuously, as though she knew her sparks were far superior to theirs.

The pace, while hardly sedate, was easy enough that Diamond could keep up without effort, and for long stretches, they kept pace alongside another dragon, Misty, who was carrying four delegates—almost as if she were a bus, Ember thought with amusement.

It wasn't until midafternoon that they were out of the mountains and skimming over an alluvial plain, braided with glistening rivers. They landed at one of the palace way-stations, looked after by a few shepherding families. This was a chance to stretch their legs and have a bite to eat. The shepherds quickly dispatched several panicked goats and threw the carcasses to the dragons, who blasted them with fire until the charred carcasses were to their liking, before snaffling them back with obvious relish.

With a growl, Diamond tore off a goat's leg and tossed it at Ember with one shake of her head. Ember dodged the flying limb, and it thudded to the ground behind her.

"I have my own lunch." She retrieved the mangled goat's leg and shoved it back at the dragon. "But thanks for the offer."

"How is she doing?" Sten asked, coming up to the pair. Diamond fixed him with a gleaming eye and dipped her head in polite acknowledgement of the One, while Ember attempted to bow and wipe her bloodied hands on her pants at the same time.

"She's doing so well." Ember was still buzzing from adrenaline, although whether that was from the excitement of the ride, the bracing air and magnificent scenery, or the Stone mage's enchantment, she couldn't say. She was fatigued, though. Flying for enjoyment around the palace grounds hadn't prepared her for such a long journey, and they weren't even out of the Stones' territory yet.

"Once we leave the rivers, we'll be in no-man's-land between us and the Swords, before heading between the grasslands and the Seeds."

Ember had assumed they would skirt the Skies territory and the grasslands, and then drop into the western desert, but Sten was adding several hundred kilometres to the trip by going the other way, not to mention putting themselves closer to the Seeds.

As if guessing what she was thinking, Sten said, "The dragons don't like to fly over water, or else we'd just circle right round the coast. I've no wish to fight with Lakin the whole way, and have him sulking all the way back. Besides, if the Seeds see us, let them shake in their little green boots. They'll know the power of the Stones."

He gave Ember a friendly clap on her shoulder and moved on to speak to some others. Ember leaned her forehead against Diamond's hide, trying to hide her weariness. Although the young dragon appeared eager to get on, Ember couldn't say the same. Even though she wore gloves and a hood, her hands and ears were almost numb with cold from blasting through the frigid mountain air, and her legs were shaky with the effort of balancing with Diamond's shifting and swooping to catch the most efficient air currents.

She couldn't relax on the dragon's back for a moment. She had to be alert for a sudden dive, an ear-popping ascent, or an abrupt turn, and she couldn't predict what Diamond was going to do, or why. Firespeech was restricted to the rulers, the heirs, and the dragon-riders, but most of the Stones could grasp a dragon's intention, if not actual words. Sten and Lakin had an extremely close bond, and Ember could see him now, laughing with Lakin, while the dragon gave him a nudge with his jaw, as if he too were amused.

It frustrated her sometimes, that things that came so easily to them were so hard for her. She was a Stone too, wasn't she? Even if she was only a half, she wanted to prove she belonged. That was why she pushed her training so much, and why she was reluctant to tell anyone how tired she was. For the first time, she wondered at the wisdom of accepting the Stones' invitation to the Sands, although she thought wryly, they didn't exactly give her the opportunity to decline.

She ate her fruit pieces, and crusty bread stuffed with meat paste, drank some sweet wine, and spent the rest of the short break stretching out her leg and bum muscles, much to the amusement of the surrounding fae who had clearly never seen a downward dog before.

When Sten announced they should move on, she settled into the saddle, which although padded and perfectly matched to her curves, felt harder and more uncomfortable than it had before, and made sure she had a firm grip, as Diamond lunged forward and took to the air again, the shepherds below bowing so low their foreheads grazed the ground.

As they flew southeast, the sparkling river threads soon gave way to the broad, fast flowing Dry, the river that bordered the northern side of Skies territory. Their towers loomed ominously, looking rather like an Earth cityscape. The Skies had been noticeably absent from the crowning of the Sword ceremonies. Only a few representatives had shown up for the contest before hastily disappearing afterwards. They'd crowned their own rulers just a few months before, following the unexpected demise of the previous pair. The Skies selected their rulers by vote from selected courtiers, and there were whispers that this election wasn't so much a democratic decision as a polite coup.

Diamond banked and banked again, keeping pace with the other dragons, who were flying in rather closer formation than before as they headed along the riverbank. This side of the Dry was a no-man's-land between the Skies and the Swords, the border a wide strip of land between each kingdom's territories where anyone might roam and none would suffer consequences. As soon as they entered the border, the quality of the air changed, became a sepia-coloured soup that dragged at the dragons' wings and made them slow and ungainly. Ahead lay a range of hills that marked the border between the Seeds and the Free Grasslands where the dragons might hunt wild game before they set off again, to get to the Sands by nightfall.

It was late afternoon now, and the sun was sinking lower in the sky. It shone directly in Ember's eyes, and even the hooded eye-guards she wore to protect her eyes from the streaming wind were no match against the bright rays. She twisted her head this way and that, wishing fruitlessly for a decent pair of sunglasses, and then cried out as Diamond plunged and sharply banked. A fizzing noise shot past Ember's shoulder and then another, and she threw herself forward, pressing her face to Diamond's scaly back to avoid the thicket of arrows—arrows the size of massive spears—which were suddenly everywhere.

The tight formation immediately split, as the fleet sought to confuse whoever was firing on them. Sten and Ruby's mounts climbed higher, disappearing into a cloud bank. Shouts and cries filled the air, but Ember couldn't tell what was happening. She could only cling on as Diamond swung this way and that, and once, horrifyingly, rolled in midair, a move which, if Ember hadn't been securely strapped in, would have sent her plummeting.

Pushing back into a sitting position, she gazed wildly around, but Diamond had entered the clouds too, and there was no visibility. There were cries from the other delegates and screeches from the dragons, but the thick atmosphere of the border muffled the sound. The clouds weren't helping either; she couldn't tell from which direction the cries were coming.

Another arrow hissed through the clouds. Diamond dodged it neatly, only to fly straight into the path of another. The dragon gave a horrifying squeal and a sticky stream of hot, red blood splattered Ember's face and torso. For one terrifying second they hung in mid-air, and then Diamond hurtled toward the ground, one wing hanging ragged and limp, the spear sticking out of the joint where her wing met her shoulder. A viscous purple liquid coated the shaft, hissing and bubbling where Diamond's blood had made contact.

"Diamond!" Her scream was torn from her lips as Diamond fell, spinning wildly, out of control. Ember clung as tightly as she could, trying to conjure a barrier which would slow their fall, but her panic and terror made it impossible. She cast a soft, insubstantial mist that slowed Diamond's descent a little, but the ground was still rushing toward them, faster and faster, and then everything went black.

Chapter 5

The darkness eventually became a misty white and a magnificent room came into focus, a couch, table and chairs placed just so, books lining the walls, arched windows covered with lacework screens shrouding the outside view, the light blazing through golden and warm.

Ashe was leaning against the doorway, and as she saw him, he came forward, took her hand and kissed the back of her knuckles, his breath warming her chilly hands. She wondered where her gloves had disappeared to, but the thought vanished just as quickly as it had arrived.

"Hello, Ember."

"Hello, Ashe."

Ashe bade her to sit on the couch, and he settled next to her. A colourful array of food, sweets, candied fruits, tiny sandwiches with delicious looking fillings, appeared on the table in front of them, but she wasn't hungry, and it faded away into nothing.

Instead, she focused on Ashe. He looked different. The expression in his eyes was watchful and sad, and his features were gaunt, his bearing weary. He smiled at her as if he hadn't smiled in a long time, as if the sun was finally shining after days of cloud, and she responded, leaning closer to him to feel its warmth.

"How is it, being the Blade?"

"I cannot ..." he paused, tried again. "My first loyalty is to the Sword."

She could guess what he meant. "So, you can't speak against her?"

He gave a tiny shake of his head and repeated, "My first loyalty is to her. Her power runs through me and mine within her. We are almost one."

"Does she know I'm here?"

"No. I can keep her from knowing for a short while. But you mustn't stay long."

Impulsively, she reached out to him and cupped his cheek. He closed his eyes and briefly clasped her hand before pulling away.

She tried not to show how his indifference made her feel and asked lightly, "Do you miss being outside?"

"It is comfortable here. Quiet. Peaceful."

She rose from the couch to look outside the window. As she drew closer, the light became dazzling and she couldn't make out much behind the lace screens other than a blazing white. "What's out there?"

"Nothing. But the mansion is vast. I doubt I shall be here long enough to explore all its secrets."

His world had shrunk to the four walls around him, and yet he didn't look as though he minded. He seemed content, if it weren't for the wistful expression in his eyes as he looked at her.

"Is ... she ... treating you well?"

She couldn't bring herself to say Serafina's name, in case it was a charm or a spell that would summon her into this serene place in all her beautiful and vicious wrath. He appeared confused by the question, but she realised quickly it wasn't what she had said, but rather, how he was going to answer it without being disloyal.

"She only uses me occasionally. She has power enough to do as she wishes, and so far, she has wished for little. But she is ... capricious in her wants. Sometimes she wants death, sometimes pleasure. Sometimes they are twisted into both. It's as though ..."

He paused and Ember prompted him, "Yes?"

"She is the sun and the moon in one."

Ember frowned, not knowing what that meant. "I don't understand."

He shrugged. "Neither do I, exactly."

They sat for a while in silence, but it wasn't an awkward silence to be filled with small, careless chatter. It was the silence of old friends, content in each other's presence, with the occasional shared smile their only communication.

Eventually, he took her hands, helping her to her feet.

"You must go now, Ember."

"Yes."

She expected him to escort her to the door and show her out, but instead, he said simply, "Wake up."

"What?"

"Wake up."

CHAPTER 6

A she's voice shattered into nothing, and the golden light of the room became a heavy darkness. Slowly, she became aware that she was very cold. Her body ached and stung all over, and she tried to fall back into nothingness again to escape the overwhelming hurt, but she couldn't. Consciousness was altogether too real.

She cracked an eye and then the other, and with a tremendous effort, pushed herself upright. She'd been thrown clear from Diamond's back, although she still had a jumble of leather straps about her, one coiled around her upper torso and neck. She was lucky she hadn't been strangled.

She untangled herself and then, with her heart in her mouth, crawled over the grass to where Diamond lay. The dragon's eyes were closed and the arrow that had pierced her shoulder had snapped off, leaving the base embedded deep inside. The flow of blood was now a congealed, sticky mess. Purple smears splattered Diamond's scales. It looked as though the stuff was corrosive, for the scales that had made contact were rotting away in sickening lumps.

She gently pushed Diamond's lolling head. "Come on, Diamond, wake up."

The dragon was still breathing, which gave Ember some comfort, although it was laboured and shallow. Frantically, she scanned the sky for any other dragons, but it was overcast now. The clouds hung low and grey, and she couldn't see anything nor hear anything other than the wind.

They had landed in a grassy gully between two rounded hills. The grass stretched away to the forest on the left, and to the right was a distant shimmer which she assumed was the Dry. The sepia colour of the border had vanished. She had no idea whose territory she was in, and there was no indication from where her attackers had come. She crouched uneasily by Diamond's side, wondering if they could see her now.

A peculiar scraping sound broke the silence. Alarmed, she scanned the area, but there was nothing. The scraping was getting louder though, and now she could feel a vague rumbling beneath her feet. Earthquake, her overwrought mind insisted, having been a veteran of many in her hometown, but there was no handy table to get under, no doorway beneath which to shelter. On the plus side, there was also nothing that could fall on her either, unless you counted Diamond.

A spray of earth hit her in the face, stinging against her grazes, and she wiped at it dazedly, still unable to grasp what was happening, even as a divot grew in the ground before her, the dirt heaping to either side. Emerging from the hole were two long sticks, tapping the ground convulsively. She watched in blank confusion at first, but soon realised two things. One, the long things weren't sticks, they were feelers, and two, they were attached to a massive, segmented body that streamed up out of the ground, higher and higher, until it was towering over her, legs clicking, eyes rolling, powerful jaws stretched to reveal rows and rows of shiny, sharp teeth.

Her mind reeled. She didn't even have the ability to scream as it lunged, not at her, but at Diamond, sinking its teeth into the dragon's flank. Diamond let out a horrific groan of pain, and blood streamed as she jerked away. She tried to snap at the centipede, but it dodged easily, going for the other flank. Its jaws snapped shut, and it tore a chunk of flesh from the dragon's side. The groan became a shriek, and at last Ember found her strength.

"Get out!" A barrier erupted from her, a solid force of energy that struck the colossal centipede front on, smashing its blood-stained teeth and thrusting it backward. Again and again, Ember flung the barrier at the centipede, bashing its face into a pulpy mess. The centipede quickly accepted defeat, slithering back into its hole. The entire event had taken less than a minute, but Ember was as exhausted as if she'd been running a marathon. Still shaking with fright and adrenalin, she let the barrier dissolve into nothing and crawled to Diamond's side.

Gently calling Diamond's name, she pressed her ear to the dragon's nostrils for the stirring of a breath deep inside. Diamond sighed heavily, and Ember jerked back, startled, afraid Diamond would reactively let forth a blast of fire, but there was nothing. As she watched, the dragon began to disappear, slowly at first, from her spiky tail, all the way up her body, as though someone was gently covering her with a blanket of mist. It only took a few seconds, and then she was gone.

Ember sat there for a moment or two in bewilderment and shock, and then tears flowed and she sobbed, her head buried in her arms. Diamond was dead. She had been shot down out of the skies and then attacked by some terrible creature of the earth, and all to serve Ember. The guilt was overwhelming, and she cried until there were no tears left.

With the last of her strength, she crawled over to the packs, harnesses, saddle and straps that Diamond had left behind, looking for her personal pack that held food and emergency supplies. She left the others as they lay, but then her gaze fell on the leather strap embossed with Diamond's name, the strap she used to belt herself to the saddle, and she picked it up and buckled it around her waist. She wanted to curl up and rest, but she didn't want to remain anywhere near that freshly dug hole in case the centipede decided to come back, exacting revenge. Wincing with pain as she slid the pack onto her shoulders, she hobbled off toward the forest as fast as she could. These windswept hills were too exposed, and she was loath to get too close to the Dry either, just in case that was the part that flowed into the Skies' territory. Perhaps it was they were who had shot those arrows.

If the dragon-riders came looking for her, they'd find the saddle, and perhaps they would guess where she'd gone. She'd just shelter in the treeline; she wouldn't go too far. And hopefully, hopefully, she thought as she moved, they wouldn't be too long.

It seemed to take a very long time to reach the welcoming shelter of the trees. As soon as she entered the forest, she felt a little more protected, with a canopy overhead and trees surrounding her, and sank to the ground in relief. Her shoulder was throbbing madly, her arms having been nearly torn out of their sockets from holding on as Diamond fell. There were a myriad of grazes and scratches all over her body, and she had a tender swelling on her head.

The package with bandages, healing balm, and a concoction for hangovers was right at the bottom of the pack. She took a swig of hangover medicine, hoping it would help, and then attended to the most urgent of her injuries, feeling aches and stings fade as the healing balm went to work.

When she was done, she rested with her back against a tree, wishing the hangover medicine would cure the anxiety churning in her gut. How long would it take the others to find her? And if they didn't come, what would she do? She couldn't exactly walk back to the Kingdom of Stones. Perhaps she should try to make for the grasslands, find her old friend Swirl, and hope the centaurs didn't kill her on sight. She couldn't imagine they'd be especially keen to see her, even if she was only half fae.

Trying to distract herself from her own useless thoughts, she rummaged in the pack and nibbled on a roll of bread. She didn't feel like eating at all, but she'd need to keep her strength up.

A loud 'caw' overhead startled her, and she quickly shoved everything back in her pack, ready to run—or at least stumble quickly—if need be, but it was nothing but a brown bird, which quickly took flight and disappeared into the forest.

Even that burst of adrenaline was draining, and she slumped back against the tree trunk, picking up the bread roll she'd dropped in her fright and forcing herself to eat every bite. She felt a little better when she'd finished, and her energy finally spent, fell into a half-doze.

But something was niggling at her, nudging at her consciousness, preventing her from falling properly asleep, and in a rush, she remembered the dream she'd had when she'd fallen and hit her head. She had been visiting Ashe inside his mansion. They had talked about nothing in particular, and then he'd told her to wake up. It had been a funny sort of dream. It had an almost tangible quality about it, and just thinking about it was enough to make her fingers tingle as she remembered touching his cheek.

But it had only been a dream. She wished fervently it *had* been real, and he was at her side once more. Tears prickled behind half-closed lids, and she blinked them back. Ashe was gone forever, and she was here, in the middle of nowhere, with gruesome creepy crawlies and enemy archers who hated dragons. Getting lost in reverie wouldn't help her in the slightest, and so she forced herself to think of practicalities.

She counted off her magical skills on her fingers. Barriers, yes. Perhaps she could make one to use as a shelter to protect her when night fell, although it would probably vanish once she was asleep. She could conjure a light, with difficulty, but at least she could see in the dark—for a short time, at least. She could camouflage herself, and she had Alena's glamour brush ... she sighed in resignation. No, she didn't. It was in one of the other packs strewn on the hillside. No matter. She had a little food and half a flask of sweet wine to drink, and there was a travelling cloak in her pack which could double as a blanket. She had two firestones, but she wasn't sure about the wisdom of building a campfire, which would act as a beacon for every living thing in the vicinity. She also had a potion in a spray bottle to disguise her scent. Many fae could smell her human blood, although not all. She was supposed to have used it at the Sands' castle, to blend in with everyone else, but it might come in handy here too.

The tree she was leaning against was tall with a smooth trunk, but there were several other trees nearby that looked fairly easy to climb. She stayed on the ground until the light faded and she was sure no one was coming for her, and then, with difficulty, selected a tree and hauled herself up to a fork in the branches. She tightly secured Diamond's strap around her and tried to go to sleep.

Chapter 7

Ember had a fitful sleep, jerking awake every hour or so, convinced she was about to tumble out of the tree. When dawn arrived, she was exhausted. She slid down, relieved her bladder, ate another bread roll which had hardened considerably overnight, drank some wine, and then reapplied healing balm anywhere that seemed to need it. She took her time with these little tasks, distracting her from wondering why the Stones hadn't arrived to rescue her, but her mind kept worrying at it like a tongue with a loose tooth. They must have realised she and Diamond were missing. Why hadn't they returned for her? Unless, she thought, unless they'd all been shot down, and were lying scattered and broken about the hillsides. The thought was alarming, and she quickly stuffed everything into her pack with the vague idea that she should go and search for them. But the memory of the centipede, its jaws gouging out bloodied flesh, was still fresh, and besides, what if their attackers were lying in wait for her?

Panic rose in her again, and she took a few breaths, trying to calm herself. First things first. She needed to find water. The wine was nearly all gone, and it wasn't much good as a thirst-quencher, anyway. The Dry was the obvious choice. If she stuck to the cover of the treeline, and headed toward the riverbank they'd flown along, she was bound to find it eventually, if not a stream or pond. Just thinking about water was enough to make her throat feel scratchy. She dithered for a few minutes more, and then, with no reason to stay, headed off.

As the morning wore on, the wind changed, and clouds drew in. Before long, a fog rolled in from the hills, dank and thick, swirling around her ankles, creeping through the trees until she was in a cotton wool cocoon, hardly able to see more than a few metres ahead.

The soil underfoot became soft and uneven, and on her next step, swallowed her boot up to her ankle. She hastily jerked it out, and decided to circle right, toward the hills, but again the thin crust of earth broke underfoot, and muddy water pooled around her feet. She was forced to retreat and go into the trees, deeper into the forest.

Breaking off a branch, she plunged it into the earth, testing it as she walked. And then, as she jabbed at a mossy clump, her stick got stuck. She yanked at it, and the mossy clump split into a mouth with several rows of very long, very shiny teeth. It chomped down on her stick, sending splinters flying.

She shrieked and tore into the trees, but forced herself to slow, peeking around a tree trunk to see if the mud thing was following. Suppressing a shudder, she scanned the area but couldn't see anything in particular for the fog swirling around. Shadows and shapes seemed to loom out of the mist, and she fancied she could hear whispers coming closer and closer.

She sank to her haunches and drew her cloak tightly about her as if it could offer protection, and then realised she'd do better to cast a barrier. Once the glossy shield was in place, she crouched within it, happy that if something leapt out of the fog, it would hit the barrier first. Opening her pack, she took out the wine flask and drank the last of it. The immediate relief of liquid in her mouth felt good, but after she swallowed, she felt thirstier than before.

Then came a drizzle of rain, drops steadily plopping on her barrier, making it virtually impossible to see through. What wouldn't she give for a windscreen wiper, she thought wryly. But instead, she dissolved the barrier and set her empty wine flask out in the rain. She cast another wider barrier, shaping it like an upside-down umbrella and funnelling the rain into her flask, thankful that she might at least have a few drops to be going on with. She had only ever cast one barrier at a time, and the effort of trying to form two was beyond her. So, she stood there under the tree, her dripping cloak over her head, wishing the blasted rain would stop.

The pitter-pat of rain in her flask gave way to more whispers in the fog, and just as she'd convinced herself the eerie breathiness was merely the wind, a petulant voice sounded quite near her, cutting through the gloom.

"I'm sick of this, Glin. let's go back."

"Not until we've filled this basket," Glin replied.

"I don't care," said the first. "They're no good wet anyhow."

Ember dissolved her barrier, grabbed her flask, and edged back to the tree, peering fruitlessly through the fog. There came the sound of footsteps on leaves nearby, and she quickly cast her camouflage enchantment, remembering to include her boots and pack as well. It was a hasty job, and if she squinted, she could see the outline of her arms and legs, but surely, with all the rain and mist, she was likely to remain unnoticed. She stood motionless, hardly daring to breathe, and soon the source of conversation came into view, appearing like a mirage before being concealed by the swirling mists again, and her heart sank.

Two fae, dressed in a familiar, soft forest green.

She had stumbled into the territory of the Seeds.

Chapter 8

I t was a split decision, and then Ember was quietly swinging her pack on her shoulders and stealing after them. Thankfully, the pattering of rain on leaves disguised any sound she might have inadvertently made, but still, she didn't want to get too close, even though the fog limited her visibility, and she was scared to lose them. The two fae clearly felt there was nothing to fear, for they kept up a steady conversation, words which Ember couldn't quite make out, but loud enough for her to follow if they occasionally dipped out of sight in the mist.

If she followed them to their village, perhaps she might discover a better way out of this jungle rather than just wandering around in circles. Perhaps she might learn something new about their plans for invading the grasslands, or if they'd clapped eyes on Cole.

Besides, she didn't want to be alone.

The two fae meandered about, in no particular hurry, and occasionally one would bend and pick something from the ground, drying it off on their tunic before dropping it into a basket. Ember learned the other one's name was Radi. She was younger than Glin, often dashing ahead before returning, impatient at having to wait for Glin to catch up.

Ember followed from tree to tree, concealing herself behind shrubs and branches. She blended in to her surroundings fairly well, but she wasn't so confident in her disguise she felt she could just blatantly wander out in the open. She couldn't let them see her. They would immediately know she was human, and the only human who had ever been to Esha in recent times had been the one who had caused all the drama in the Kingdom of Swords, their allies. They would probably consider her an enemy. Hastily, she fumbled in her pack as she went, searching for the bottle of potion to disguise her scent. Sprinkling it over herself, it didn't smell like anything in particular, and she couldn't tell if it had worked. She just had to hope.

The fae wandered about for ten minutes or so, and Ember was just beginning to feel the struggle of keeping up her camouflage enchantment when Glin and Radi passed through a thicket of trees... and vanished.

Ember caught up to where she'd last seen them, looking around her in consternation. She was at the edge of a large, open clearing. There was no fog, no rain. No Glin or Radi either. And then she heard a laugh coming from somewhere overhead. She looked up, and her mouth dropped.

Above the lower canopy were glimpses of swooping walkways upon which several fae hastened, light-footed and sure, through the trees. Lights gleamed high above, like constellations of glittering stars amongst the leaves, and there were windows and doors set into some of the bigger trees.

She couldn't help moving further forward, gaping at the sight above her, and only recalling where she was when she stood on a dry stick that cracked like a pistol shot. Under the canopy it was perfectly dry underfoot, although if she looked back through the trees, she could still see a steady downpour, and fog swirling throughout the rest of the forest.

Hastily she retreated from the clearing and around a cluster of bushes, hoping the sound of her footsteps hadn't been overheard, and almost immediately tripped over a group of female fae sitting in a circle on the other side, holding hands, eyes closed. Ember held her breath, tiptoed back around the bushes and closed her eyes, trying to still the thudding of her heart.

A low chanting piqued her interest, and she crouched, peeking through the leaves to see what they were doing. She couldn't understand the words, although she felt that if she really focused on them, perhaps she might glean their meaning. There was something about it that teased her memory, as though it was a tune that she vaguely remembered from long ago. They were swaying now, back and forth with the rhythm. A basket lay in the middle of the circle, and a shower of golden sparks erupted from it, showering them all with a golden rain.

The sparks died, and the fae opened their eyes. All looked dazed, as though they were waking from sleep, but they seemed content. A fae wearing a necklace of colourful feathers, her wrists encircled with fresh flower bracelets, leaned forward and drew the basket to her. She dipped her hand in and brought out a golden snake, which immediately coiled its long length around her arm. She held the head close to her face and its tongue darted out, almost touching her. It hissed, showing golden fangs.

The fae next to her leaned closer, one hand holding a flask, the other hand hovering behind the snake's head. She grabbed it just as it struck, forcing it to release its venom into the flask. The fluid poured down the side of the flask in a golden stream, which gradually lessened as the flask filled. When there was no more, the snake rapidly withered to a husk, which desiccated further into dust. The first fae blew the dust off her arm, and it swirled around the group before dissipating into nothing.

"Well done, everyone." She deposited a kiss on the forehead of the fae who had grabbed the snake. "Another to add to the magor's stores."

The recipient of the kiss responded with a smile that looked more weary than pleased, and corked the flask, stowing it somewhere about her person.

Ember started as Radi and Glin came forward. She hadn't even noticed they had been standing nearby, watching the proceedings. Glin proffered their basket.

The first fae looked at them. "What have you?"

Glin kept her eyes on the ground. "Roidan."

The fae in the circle groaned.

"I'm too tired," one complained. "It's such a lot of effort for stupid blisters."

"Marching soldiers need remedies too," Radi piped up. She'd spoken with no hint of insolence, but the one who had complained immediately stood and slapped Radi across the face.

It had all happened so quickly that Ember gave an outraged squeak, before clapping a hand across her mouth. She edged backward, certain that she was about to find herself in the middle of a fae brawl, but Radi just retreated to stand next to Glin. The slap mark showed red against her skin, but she didn't cradle it, or burst into tears, or even so much as look at Glin for sympathy. A distinct air of boredom and detached superiority permeated her entire being, her weight resting on one leg as though she were casually lounging against a wall. It was, Ember thought, with a gleam of amusement, the classic belligerent stance of a teenager, an attitude designed to infuriate.

The one who had slapped her flushed with fury. Through gritted teeth, she repeated, "I'm too tired for blisters."

The first reprimanded her. "Sit down and do your duty."

Studying Glin and Radi, Ember noted they differed in appearance to those seated on the ground. Besides the plain, narrow cut of their clothing, which was in sharp contrast to the decorated, elaborate outfits of the others, the ones sitting had a similar look to them: long, straight dark hair, a soft brown hue to their skins, pointed ears, and eyebrows that were barely there, whereas Radi and Glin had creamy complexions with sharp, dark eyebrows, and curly hair that looked similar to Ember's when she let it grow long.

The first addressed herself to Glin. "You may go. Be ready for the evening meal."

As the two fae made themselves scarce, the others resumed their places, with the basket of roidan in the centre. This time, their chanting brought forth a shower of black sparks from the basket. Ember didn't stay for the rest; she headed off after Glin and Radi. They were servants or slaves, and those behind the scenes always knew everything.

She caught up with them on the other side of the clearing. They hurried, not up a tree as she had been half-hoping, for she longed to see what it was like so high up there, but down a well-worn dirt track, which led to another clearing.

Here was a series of rough huts created from branches and large leaves. They must have been held together by arcane means, for Ember couldn't see nails or flax string, or anything binding one support to another. The two fae went swiftly to the rear of the buildings and sat at a bench with a long table. Food appeared out of thin air, a large wooden platter with a selection of fruit and meat. The two retrieved a piece each and nibbled, clearly trying to make the morsels last as long as possible.

"I'm glad we're first back," Radi said. "I'm starving."

"Just one piece, though."

"I know, I know."

Ember edged closer until she was at the corner of a hut, just out of sight.

"They'll need a remedy for blisters more than they'll know," remarked Glin.

Radi chuckled. "Far more than a golden potion of prophecy. What would a Seed know about prophecy compared to a centaur? I don't even know why they're bothering. None of them want this war."

"Keep your voice down," Glin admonished. "Or you'll earn yourself another slap, from me."

There was a brief silence and then Radi said, "I hope when they look into the future they'll see that their campaign is doomed. And when that happens, mother, we must be ready to flee."

She spoke in such a low voice, Ember had to inch even closer to her to hear what she was saying. Glin cried out, and she and Radi leapt to their feet, looking around the clearing and then at each other. Excitement was writ plain on their faces as Glin held out her hand.

She was wearing a ring, a glowing golden stone set in tarnished silver. It was worn and old, and Ember couldn't think why they were fixated on it. And then her own attention was diverted as a large black and red insect zoomed past her face, making a threatening buzzing sound. She flinched, waving a hand ineffectually, and it turned and came for her again, apparently seeing right through her camouflage. She swiped at it, inching backward. It was impossible to focus on her concealment with a loud buzzy thing intent on dive-bombing her face, and the enchantment flickered in and out, her body reappearing and disappearing again.

"Wait," Radi said, her tone disappointed. "It's stopped."

"But it was there. You saw it."

"You should put it in your pocket. If they see it …"

The insect dived again, and Ember lashed out, neatly tripping over a water butt and falling to the ground with a muffled oath. The insect immediately landed on her forearm and sank a sharp stinger into her flesh. She yelped with pain, slapped it and flicked the crushed body away.

"What was that?"

It was too late to run. Both Glin and Radi appeared, looking down at Ember's flickering body in amazement, and eventually she gave up the subterfuge with a snort of exasperation, a rueful shrug and a little wave.

"Hey ya."

CHAPTER 9

The two fae seemed to have lost the power of speech. Neither looked scared nor alarmed, but still Ember rose slowly, palms facing outward in a sign of conciliatory peace. "I'm so sorry. I was lost."

Without hesitation, Glin pounced, grabbing her wrist. Ember tried to jerk free, but Glin twisted her arm and dragged her close, peering at the skin where the insect had bitten her. The red puncture wound was rapidly turning purple, the flesh around it beginning to swell.

"A badgebug got you," Glin said.

"I've got some stuff in my pack." Almost immediately, a wave of dizziness came over Ember, and Glin slid an arm around her waist to steady her.

Radi grabbed her pack, fishing through it quickly and finally held up a bottle of Ember's healing balm. "This?" Without waiting for a reply, she undid the stopper and sniffed. She shook her head. "I don't know what this is."

She held it out to Glin, who sniffed and shrugged. Radi stuffed the bottle back in the pack and bounded off into the trees. Ember watched, not really comprehending what was happening. Her throat was constricting, and she was finding it hard to swallow. Black spots danced in front of her eyes. She held out her hand for the bottle, but Glin shook her head.

"There's only one thing good for badgebug bite, and that's not it. Hold on, dearie, Radi won't be a moment."

Ember blinked slowly. Stinging needles jabbed her arm, working their way up to her shoulder, and Glin was alternately growing larger and smaller, as though her head was a balloon being blown up, and then the air forced out again. It seemed forever before Radi came out of the forest clutching a handful of leaves. She stuffed them in her mouth and chewed, and then spat the resulting mess on Ember's arm. The green mass was full of tiny white bubbles and smelled like rotten fruit. Glin rubbed it in with gentle fingers and the prickling stabs faded.

"Thank you," Ember croaked. Glin's head may have resumed its normal size, but Ember's throat still felt stuffed with cotton wool.

"Up there." Radi pointed to an overhang on the hut. A conical sack-like nest clung to the wooden post, and a red and black badgebug sat on top, eyeing the action below with a decided air of satisfaction, Ember thought.

"Lucky you found it first," Glin said. "We'll have to burn it. But first ..." her tone turned grim. "Who are you?"

Belatedly, Ember realised she should really have rehearsed a back-story. Her mind was still befuddled enough that she couldn't think of a decent lie, so she settled on omission instead.

"I'm Ember. I got lost on my way to the Dry. Could you please show me the way out?"

Radi gave an ugly bark of laughter. "The way out? There is no way out." At the look of alarm on Ember's face, she added, "For us, I mean. But for you?" she pointed through the trees. "The Dry is that way."

"Thank you. And thank you for ..." she showed them her arm. The swelling was fading, but the skin was still blotchy and prickling in waves. "I'll have to find some of those leaves."

Glin's expression was wary. "Where are you from? I've not seen someone dressed like ..."

She gestured at Ember's outfit, which was still mostly covered by her travelling cloak, but there was a peek of her suede tunic and pants underneath, the easy style preferred by the Stones, the fabric warm but allowing the skin to breathe.

Ember wasn't sure what to say and hoped her hesitation would be interpreted as wooziness from the insect sting rather than reluctance. From what they had said, and from their appearance, she suspected they weren't of the Seeds themselves. Certainly, they had shown no love for the fae with whom they lived.

"A long way away. I was part of a group, but we got separated."

Radi gasped. Her eyes grew round, and she edged ever so slightly toward Glin.

"Would you be part of the Stones' contingent, then?" Glin asked, bluntly. "The Seeds shot one of them out of the sky. By the time they found the courage to look for them, they'd gone. Everyone presumed a garakworm had eaten them."

She nodded. "Yeah. That was me."

Radi sucked in a breath. "You rode a dragon?"

Just thinking about Diamond made Ember's eyes prickle. "She was only young. It was her first journey with the fleet."

Glin shushed Radi's attempt to ask another question, and said, "And tell me why I shouldn't just drag you to the elders right now?"

Ember's mind was still muddled, and she couldn't think of a response, except a saying she'd heard long ago. "Because the enemy of my enemy is my friend?"

Glin's lips pursed, her eyes narrowed and for a moment, Ember thought she'd made a terrible mistake, but then Glin broke into a grudging smile. "Well, you've got nerve, I'll give you that."

Voices drifted into the clearing, and Radi turned pale. "Quick."

She grabbed Ember's pack, and she and Glin hustled Ember between the huts to a small one at the rear. Glin pushed her through the door and threw her pack in after her. "Stay there and stay quiet. And don't be tempted to try your disguise. Badgebug venom interferes with magic for ages. We'll come and get you."

The door clicked shut, and Ember, still dizzy and shaken by their abrupt retreat, sank on a chair and took stock of her surroundings. There wasn't much. A small bed, the hard wooden chair upon which she sat, a low bench with a bowl and a jug of water, and a wooden chest underneath. But when she looked up, she drew in a delighted breath. Hanging from the ceiling was a garden of flowers. Not dried flowers, but fresh, blooming flowers of all colours that grew upside down from the mossy green rafters and filled the room with the delicious scent of summer roses and lavender.

She rested for a while. Her arm still felt weird, and she had a headache. She applied a few drops of healing balm to her skin, but Glin had been right about its efficacy; it made little difference. But with time, the pain eased, and her mind became clear again. She peeked out the window, but there was nothing to see except the hut next door.

The waiting grated, and anxiety began to build. What was she waiting for, anyway? They'd told her which way the Dry lay. The longer she hung around, the greater her chances of discovery.

She swung her pack on her back and eased open the door, sticking her head out. Huts loomed on either side, their dark windows like staring eyes, making her feel uneasy. She tried casting her camouflage enchantment, and it worked for a moment or two, but then slid away. She gave it another attempt, and again she couldn't make it stick.

"Stupid badgebug," she muttered, promising herself the next time she packed for a trip, a can of insect repellent was going to be first in the bag.

She gently latched the door behind her and moved quietly between the huts. Voices and the occasional burst of laughter carried on the breeze, but it sounded weary and stilted. She supposed they were all servants here, just finishing their afternoon work and preparing for the evening shift. If these fae were anything like the Swords' servants, their evening duties would extend into the night, catering to dinners and entertainments. This would be the best chance to depart, while all were resting and occupied with their dinner.

Keeping her head down, she moved swiftly in the direction of the Dry, taking a track between the huts, which led to a series of large boxes on smooth stilts. They were only large enough to fit a small child, and woven baskets were stacked within. Food storage, she assumed, built in such a way to keep out rats and other scavenging animals. Finally, she came to the thick forest of trees that marked the boundary of the settlement. The fog had cleared somewhat, but the rain was still falling.

Damn.

She pulled her hood over her head and darted out into the rain. It was much cooler out here too, and she quickened her pace, hoping that she'd feel warmer with the exercise. But she couldn't keep it up for long. Her body had undergone much trauma in the past few days and she couldn't sustain a pace much more than a lope, which soon became a hobbling walk.

Still, at least she was heading in the right direction.

But it wasn't long before she heard quick, pattering footsteps behind her and, heart pounding, she spun to see Radi heading toward her.

Ember halted, wishing she'd thought to put her dagger in her belt, and held up her fists in a boxing stance instead. "Don't come any closer," she warned. "I'll fight you."

Radi laughed, a pealing chime incongruous with the gloomy forest and rainy drizzle. "Don't be silly. You couldn't fight a fly."

"I have to go."

"I know. I just came to bring you this."

She held out a hand, showing Ember a crusty roll of bread with a strip of meat sticking out from the middle.

"Thank you," said Ember, touched, for she remembered how Glin had admonished Radi to only take one piece of food from the servants' platter. "That's very kind."

She took the bread and stuffed it in her pocket.

"The enemy of my enemy is my friend," Radi said, her expression serious.

"So, you're not a Seed then? I didn't think so. Where did you come from?"

Radi's expression was watchful, cautious, as though she wasn't sure if she could trust Ember, and Ember nodded encouragingly, smiling. Finally, Radi spoke, her voice low. "I come from the Shields."

CHAPTER 10

E mber wasn't sure she'd heard correctly. "The Shields? Really?"

Radi nodded, growing expansive with Ember's obvious interest. "My great-grandmother was a Shield. She escaped the wars and ended up in Seeds territory with a bunch of others. They caught her and made her a servant, so, well, here I am."

"I thought all the Shields were destroyed."

"They wished. But not all." She fixed Ember with a sharp gaze, reminding Ember of a bird intent on a worm. "You know nothing about us?"

"No. Just that the war forced the Swords to treaty, and—"

"Ugh," Radi's tone was scathing. "Swords."

Ember grinned, and Radi smiled shyly back.

"I don't suppose you know about the heir of the Swords visiting the Seeds territory?" She couldn't hope that Radi would have actually seen Cole; their settlement was on the outskirts, but perhaps she had heard something.

Radi shook her head. "News travels slowly here, and the rulers live far away, by the archipelago. That's where he'd go. Not here, at the arse-end of the world." She looked as though she wanted to keep Ember talking, but the light was fading and Ember was eager to get moving again.

"I'd better go now," she said.

"I know." Radi pointed through the trees. "See the starstones? They lead to the Dry."

Ember looked, blinked, looked again. A line of glowing white mushrooms had appeared, a phosphorescent signpost showing the way. She wouldn't have even noticed them if Radi hadn't pointed them out, and she thanked her gratefully.

"Was it wonderful? Riding a dragon?" Radi's eyes sparkled.

"Yes. Yes, it was. Perhaps you can travel to the mountains one day and see for yourself."

Radi's face fell. "That's not going to happen."

"I don't know about that," said Ember, lightly. "If a Shield can get to the Seeds, what's stopping her from getting to the Stones?"

Radi lit up, a gleam of hope in her dark eyes, and for an instant, Ember could see the adult she would grow to be, strong, resolute, determined. "Goodbye. Good luck."

Ember took her hand, squeezed it gently, and moved off. When she glanced back over her shoulder, Radi had gone.

As the evening wore on, the rain finally stopped. She was gratified she could move faster, not wanting to be caught in the middle of the jungle after dark. When she'd been on those windswept hills, she'd been certain she'd be safer in the jungle, and now she was desperate to see the back of it.

The starstones glowed brighter as the sun dropped and the shadows lengthened, and she was glad of them. She startled more than once at the unfamiliar chirruping of night insects and scuffling of small animals, and once, there came a low growl that sent her scrambling for the nearest tree, wishing again she'd thought to put her dagger in a place where she could easily get to it. As soon as she was ensconced on a high branch, she fumbled in her pack for it, and thrust it into her belt loops.

She squinted through the foliage, searching for the thing that growled so menacingly. A bird gave a loud squawk to sound an alarm, and the forest fell silent. Even the insects stopped their low rhythmic chirping. In the uneasy silence, there came a glimpse of something, no, the *shadow* of something, slinking through the trees, as fluid as liquid, sliding around trunks and between bushes, before vanishing into the undergrowth. Ember held her breath, and soon the forest sounds resumed, hesitantly at first, and then with as much vigour as before.

Hopefully, the thing had gone. Hopefully, it hadn't caught her scent and was waiting somewhere down there, out of sight, for her to climb down again. She wasn't in any particular hurry to find out. Instead, she took out the bun Radi had given her and bit into it, relishing the spiced meat in the middle. It was very juicy, she thought idly, and as she looked at it more closely, she almost gagged. It wasn't juice; it was blood. The meat was raw.

She chewed again, her nose wrinkling, but loath to spit out a perfectly good mouthful that might make the difference between her survival or not, and concluded that although it was raw, it still tasted pretty good. *Steak tartare,* she thought. *Just like a fancy restaurant.*

She wasn't keen to climb down again just yet, but noted uneasily that the longer she waited, the longer the shadows stretched, and turned her mind to Radi's surprising announcement. A descendant of the Shields! When Ashe and Cole had talked about the war, Ember had assumed it had happened centuries ago, and not a mere four generations, but of course, the fae were long lived. She'd also assumed that the Shields had all been wiped out, their lands destroyed. Perhaps it was just the ruling family who had been eradicated, with the common folk choosing escape rather than death. How unfortunate that they'd landed in the lap of their enemy's ally. But perhaps there were other Shields out there, blending with the other kingdoms, trying not to draw attention to themselves. Perhaps some of them were still free, still waiting for their time to return to their homeland, just as the centaurs had. It was odd, that neither Ashe nor Cole had mentioned that there were Shields' fae out there in the world. Surely they knew the Seeds harboured some of them, even if only as servants? And if not, why not? Were the Seeds keeping that a secret? She sighed. Understanding Esha politics was like untangling a ball of knotted string, and it was even worse with a banging headache.

She peered down through the branches again, but not seeing anything untoward, dropped gracelessly from the tree and attempted a camouflage charm. Slowly, she took on the colours of the surrounding forest. It wasn't fully solid and the outline of her body seemed obvious to her, but it was better than nothing.

Travelling in the dark sucked. More than once, overhanging branches clocked her on the head, and more than once, she almost turned her ankles on the thick veins of tree roots underfoot. Every noise she made seemed to be magnified, and so she tried to move carefully, stifling the heavy sound of her breathing. Her camouflage improved as the minutes passed, which, although comforting, was also a problem in itself. Her legs weren't visible, so she couldn't see how high she had to tread, and was constantly tripping over ruts and logs. The sooner she was free of this damn jungle, the better.

She rounded a tree trunk and then stopped in consternation. The line of glowing starstones had vanished. She turned, intending to head back to the previous one to see if she'd taken a wrong turn, but stopped. She'd glimpsed bright yellow eyes quite low to the ground, and the gleam of white teeth. The glowing mushroom promptly disappeared in two halves, as though bitten once and then twice.

Hastily she put the tree trunk between her and it, hoping the thing would follow the starstones back from where she had come. She didn't care if it was eating the ones she'd already passed. But to her horror, the stealthy slither of flesh against leaves was approaching. She risked a peek. The thing's eyes were rising off the ground, higher and higher. She'd imagined it as a python, but it would be standing on the base of its tail if it were. Ember watched it, her head tilting back, clapping a hand over her mouth to remind herself not to scream. It turned this way and that.

It knows I'm here, she thought frantically. *It's looking for me.*

She shrank back against the tree trunk, forgetting she still had her pack on her back. The leather rubbed against the bark and immediately the thing turned, slamming into the tree, hissing with fury.

Ember took off, her pack banging against her shoulder blades. She had no idea which way she was supposed to be going anymore. Her only thought was to get as far away from that snake thing as she could. But she had barely taken twenty steps when she tripped over a tree root and crashed onto the ground.

Dazed, she rolled onto her side, hands raised to create the barrier that she was usually so good at, but it appeared only as a splotch of filmy egg white before dissolving into nothing.

The shadow loomed up over her, and she screamed.

Chapter 11

T he echo of her scream ringing in her ears faded, and Ashe said calmly, "The thing is, it's not about strength, or force of will. It's about concentration. And you can't do that if you're distracted."

"Thanks a lot," Ember said drily. "That's very helpful."

Golden light filled the room, a room with a long mahogany table marching down the centre, covered with maps and little silver miniatures placed here and there: centaurs, winged fae, castles, tiny dragons. Ashe stood at one end, carelessly tossing what looked like a long croupier stick from hand to hand. Abruptly, he laid the stick on the table and came toward her, his hand reaching to caress her face. She closed her eyes, waiting for the electric jolt, the recognition that her soul felt when his touched hers, the flicker of passion he always engendered within her, but he paused, his hand a mere hairsbreadth away from her skin.

"Don't think about anything else. Fill yourself with your task and allow nothing to come between you and your goal."

"Anything else?" She leaned toward him, longing for the touch of his flesh on hers.

"Yes. Wake up."

Ember opened her eyes. The thing was poised above her as though it had been waiting for her, and she slammed up her barrier just as it struck. It cannoned into the unyielding skin of her bubble and let out a screech of pain and fury as it crumbled into dust. The breeze whipped the dust across the leaves, making a pattering sound like raindrops, and then it was gone.

The barrier dissolved, and Ember raised herself up on her elbows. For just the briefest moment, she'd imagined a scent on the wind, a delicious, heady perfume of spices and honey, and then it had faded, along with a strange memory of golden light and a feeling of utter calm and safety. And then she saw a glowing mushroom growing just beyond.

With a groan, for she felt as though she had been just one big ache for days now, she shakily got to her feet, adjusted her pack, and followed the rest of the starstone trail the thing hadn't got around to eating. Soon the trees thinned, the scent of fresh grass filled the air, and she finally saw the stars in the open night sky.

She had no intention of making for the river in the pitch black, and she couldn't tell if any nearby trees were suitable for climbing. And so she crawled into a mass of bushes, finding a dry patch underneath. She covered herself with her cloak, hoping that she looked like just another bump on the ground. Sleep came as if she'd had been hit over the head with a hammer. Her body and mind had suffered so much that it couldn't cope with anything else but a complete unconscious break from reality to repair and renew.

She dreamed of nothing.

A riot of jubilant birdsong woke her, and she snuggled deeper into her cloak, disinclined to face the day ahead. But eventually, she had to relieve her prickling bladder, and she resentfully dragged herself up and squatted. There were still a few crumbs of food at the bottom of her pack and a little water in her wine flask from the rainstorm the day before and after she'd had both, she felt better.

Now that Ember was truly awake, she could see the treeline stretching away to left and right, and the open fields with tall grasses swaying in the breeze. Far to the south lay a glimpse of sparkling water, many kilometres away. She stuck to the treeline, not wanting to go into the trees in case she was accosted by a walking snake, and not wanting to go out into the fields in case a centipede—what was it Glin had called it? A garakworm?—erupted up through the ground. Was there nowhere she could feel safe?

As she walked, she tried to formulate a plan. She'd have to cross the Dry to get into the Sands territory. And then she just had to cross a desert to find a disappearing castle, with no food, no shelter, and no compass. Easy peasy, she thought. Alright, so the long-range plan was stupid. She'd have to shrink it down, bring it back to the first step, getting to the Dry. That was going to take ages at the rate she was going. Her pace would be even slower once hunger really took hold. With a vague sense of accomplishment, she decided she would walk for an hour or so, whilst looking for something to eat. Like what? She had no idea which plants were edible. And she only had her dagger. She'd have to catch wild game barehanded before she could stab it.

She frowned. Her training lessons at the Stones suddenly seemed woefully inadequate. She should have learned a charm to attract game or to persuade a cloud to rain. Those may have proved difficult, though. She'd struggled with many of the charms even the children found easy. She couldn't draw intricate patterns onto stone with just her finger, and she couldn't read the marked stones that foretold practical things like the upcoming weather or if anyone was coming to visit. The rune markings jumped back and forth, twisting and turning so that she couldn't read them properly. She'd assumed she had some kind of rune dyslexia, and she hadn't bothered trying to force it. Instead, she concentrated on those enchantments she was good at: casting barriers, camouflaging herself, using an invisible force to push others away. Kalin had always said her power was odd, as if it were trying to make itself to do things that were unnatural to it, but of course her human blood would interpret anything fae as strange.

She continued on, trying to forget her upcoming hunger and when her stomach rumbled, she ignored that too. The sun grew higher, and she sat and rested, using her pack as a pillow. She fell into an uneasy doze in the shade of the trees, and when something noisily scampered through the forest behind her, she sat bolt upright, hand on her dagger, but there was nothing, and so she hoisted her pack on her back and continued on.

The tantalising sparkle of the Dry disappeared as the incline rose. She panted, her muscles straining as she climbed a hill, and her heart sank when she reached the top, the rumpled view of the countryside around her. The jungle cut a foreboding dark line against the countryside, and she could make out the sheer cliffs of a steep gorge far to the east. The Dry wound between hills to the south, and it was further than she had initially thought. Much further. She sat for a while on the summit, and then, telling herself with a forced cheerfulness that it was all downhill from here, started down the hill, one plodding foot after another.

It took two more hills before she called it quits. She found a little hollow beneath some trees and nestled into it, swallowing the last of the water, which did little for her thirst but awakened the gnawing hunger she'd ignored while walking. It wasn't evening yet, but she was exhausted, and it wasn't long before she went to sleep.

In the morning, she woke with a raging headache and aching limbs. A light covering of dew had fallen, and she licked every flat leaf she could find, hoping the misted foliage would alleviate her thirst. When she squatted to relieve herself, her urine was so dark yellow it was almost brown.

She walked only an hour before having to rest. It was cold, and she burrowed into her cloak, thankful for its warmth. She sat for a long time, unmoving, wondering what to do. She'd probably just die out here, another victim of the great outdoors. If thirst didn't get her, hypothermia probably would. She remembered reading about hypothermia victims, how they had a tendency to lose their minds at the end, casting aside their clothes in the mistaken belief they were burning up, and she grinned without humour at the thought of running around the hills in the nuddy before likely being gobbled up by a garakworm.

A rustle in the undergrowth alerted her to something lurking nearby, and she froze, casting a vague camouflage that merely toned her skin and clothing to the pale green of the grass underneath her. Crawling stealthily through the grass like a hunting cat, she carefully parted the grass stalks to reveal a pigeon with glossy green feathers and a white breast, feeding on a cluster of seed stalks. It saw her as soon as she saw it, but only managed a few waddling steps before she pounced, her hunger making her far more agile than she usually was. She promptly wrung its neck, her usual squeamishness at such a task replaced with a burst of pride. She felt like doing a war cry.

Returning to her pack, she ripped off feathers as fast as she could, the downy fluff descending upon her pack, cloak, hair and eyelashes in a fine cloud. She was too hungry to make a proper job of it, reasoning they would just burn off in the fire anyway, and then hunted for dry wood. She dug a little trench, piled it high with twigs, and retrieved the firestones from their velvet-lined box in her pack. They weren't stones as such, but two fae-made globes that created sparks when clacked together. After several frustrating minutes trying to make the sparks go toward the trench rather than her bare arms, the dry twigs burst into flame, and she carefully laid a few heavier sticks on top. While the fire took, she gutted the bird, and then shoved a damp green branch through it, carefully balancing it over her fire.

Burning feathers did not smell at all nice.

Ember was too hungry to wait long and ate the bird while it was still a little bloody in the middle, telling herself that salmonella probably didn't exist in this world, and besides, her hangover cure would take care of an upset stomach in a jiffy. As much as she wanted to devour the whole thing, she made herself save half, wrapping the carcass in leaves and stowing it in her pack. She stamped out the fire and tried to clean her hands on the grass before giving up and deciding she could nap just as well with sticky hands as without, and, finding a sheltered corner beneath some bushes, promptly fell asleep.

She continued on her way in the early afternoon, feeling much better about the world in general. The clouds had retreated, the temperature was pleasant, and the next hill was far enough away that she didn't have to think about toiling up it just yet.

A couple of birds, agitated by her presence, broke into a loud trilling, and she ducked with a curse as they promptly dive-bombed her. She swatted fruitlessly at them, whilst keeping an eye out for the nest they were obviously guarding, and found it nestled in a slight depression in the grass ("stupid place for a nest," she told them), before stealing two brown eggs, leaving the rest for the parents, and eating them raw.

When she finally reached the base of the hill, she was delighted to find a little waterfall gushing onto the rocks below, with the stream disappearing off into the forest. The water was clear and icy fresh. She drank and drank and then removed her clothing, crouched under the tinkling falls and washed.

Sundown wasn't for a couple more hours, and she was reluctant to leave the stream behind. Instead, she lit a small fire, placed a couple of river rocks in its heart, and then experimented with casting a barrier in the stream to catch a few darting fish. They swam into the V-shaped trap, and she closed the end, turning it into a bubble. Carefully, she lifted it out of the stream and floated it toward her, admiring the way the sun reflected through the water, making the fish look like flecks of flashing silver. She dissolved the barrier, stupidly dousing herself with water in the process, the fish flipping back and forth helplessly on the grass. The fire had died down, but the rocks were hot enough for cooking. She dropped the fish on top, retrieving them when cooked with the flat of her dagger.

Survival, she thought, was easy.

And then she was thrown backward to the ground in a flash of white-hot agony as an arrow slammed into her.

CHAPTER 12

Pain exploded in Ember's shoulder and blossomed outward, leaving her fingers numb, her chest tightening in a muscle spasm so fierce, she thought she might be having a heart attack. She couldn't bring herself to look at the shaft of wood sticking out of her shoulder, but she could feel it against tentative, bloodied fingertips, the bones of her shoulder grating as she shuffled into a sitting position, trying to see who the fuck had shot her.

There came the sound of galloping hooves and through eyes streaming with pain and fear, she saw several centaurs racing toward her, arrows already drawn for a second assault.

She tried to conjure a barrier, but her brain wasn't cooperating. That part of her mind so good at keeping her safe was utterly failing her. She couldn't bring the tatters of thought together to form a cohesive defence, and instead she held her hand up, as if that would do any good.

"No, please —" she cried, but her voice was a husky croak, and even the act of speaking sent another jolt of pain through her, making her throat close up.

"You're trespassing," one called, almost lazily, as they drew closer. "Not that it matters."

His hair was a glossy brown mane that rippled in the sunlight, the muscles of his chest and arms flexing and tautening as he raised his bow. His golden-brown eyes glittered as they met hers, and she only had enough strength to mouth the words again, "Please," before she fell back, the earth suddenly feeling as soft as a feather mattress as the darkness closed in around her.

She opened her eyes with a groan of pain as she was jolted back and forth. She was lying on the back of a covered cart, glimmers of sunlight falling between the rough weft and warp weaving of a brown cloth. Her mouth was sticky and dry, and she winced as another jolt sent a sharp pain through her shoulder.

Gingerly, she turned her head and saw a rough bandage had replaced the bloodied arrow shaft. A sigh of relief escaped her. If they were fixing her up, it meant they weren't about to kill her. Not now, at any rate.

The brown cloth lifted at one side, and a face peered in, not the centaur who had been ready to kill her, but someone else, smaller, with dark hair, who looked vaguely familiar, although with the shifting shadows and sunlight, she couldn't tell exactly who it was.

"You're awake then?" he said. "Rest easy. Rohane thought you were a Seed, but I knew who you were. Do you remember me?"

"I'm not sure. I'm sorry." Her voice was husky, barely a whisper.

"I'm Belouth. You took us out of the Swords' dungeons. And now I'm taking you home."

The words cut through her and she struggled to sit, frantic to explain. "Not to the Swords, please, not there!"

"Hush, now." His voice was warm, soothing. "Not to the Swords. Stars know I'll never set foot in that misbegotten kingdom ever again. Nay, we're taking you back to the chiron."

"I was supposed to be going to the Sands," she murmured, but he had already let the cloth fall, the rumble of the cart swallowing up her words.

She fell into an uneasy doze, her arm throbbing and preventing her from complete sleep, and she couldn't get comfortable on the wooden boards and thin layer of hay. She would have used her healing balm, but her pack had disappeared, and so she gritted her teeth, unable to stop herself from weeping when the pain got too bad.

The travel seemed to last forever, and when the wagon finally drew to a halt, she was lying in a feverish doze, her skin dry and hot. She felt strong arms lifting her from the cart, but she couldn't seem to focus on anything, faces blurring around her. The familiar smells of horse, sweat, charcoal and the distinctive rangy scent of centaur were familiar, piercing her muddled thoughts and giving her a sense of safety and calm. She was laid on something soft, and she cried out as fingers probed at her torn flesh. Eventually, a cup of sweet liquid was pressed to her lips, and she drank gratefully.

When sleep came, it did so with the blow of a hammer, thrusting her into a dream of a cavernous pit lined with flames that grew hotter and hotter as she fell toward them, and now she was on fire, her very bones igniting ...

She opened her eyes. The pain in her shoulder had eased to a dull ache, but she could still feel faint prickles of heat all over her body.

"You had a fever, but I think it's broken." It was a voice she recognised, low and gentle, and she gave a tremulous smile.

"Swirl. It's good to see you."

"I've seen you look better."

She laughed and then winced as her shoulder throbbed in warning. She was in a conical shaped hut, the roof woven in a complicated pattern with dried reeds, the floor beneath her tiles of hardened clay etched with a waving pattern that looked as though traced with a comb. A pottery bowl and jug stood in the corner, a stack of hay in the opposite corner, and a trunk with leather straps leaned against one wall. She was lying on a simple stretcher, and the blanket underneath her was luxuriously thick, fleecy and warm.

"Where's my pack? There's healing balm in it."

Just a dab and the pain would vanish as the wound closed, with scar tissue forming before nightfall. If she kept using it, the scar would fade altogether.

Swirl shook his head. "Your fae things were destroyed. You're lucky Belouth recognised you, or you would have been dealt the same fate."

"I was with some of the Stones. We were on a diplomatic mission to the Sands. But my dragon, my Diamond ... she ..."

"We saw the Seeds shoot her down. If they hadn't, we would have."

He didn't appear angry, rather, matter-of-fact. Ember struggled to sit, but her arm wasn't in any position to allow that, and so she collapsed back on the stretcher.

"But we were going to help you. The Stones were to persuade the Sands not to join the Seeds in their war."

Swirl shrugged. "I doubt it was out of love for us. Fae do what fae must to further fae interests."

Ember happened to agree with him, but she persisted. "If the outcome is peace, not war, surely it doesn't matter what their motives are? I don't even think the Seeds want war."

Swirl's heavy eyebrows lowered. "What makes you say that?"

"I overheard some of them."

"Common folk never want war. They just want to live their lives in peace, raising children so they can have their own, not raising their children for the grave. But they will fight, with the Swords egging them on."

"And guess what? They've captured Shields and use them as servants. Did you know about that?"

To her surprise, Swirl didn't show either surprise or interest. "I have no doubt there are Shields common folk living all over Esha, keeping to themselves, trying not to draw attention."

"It doesn't seem fair that they can't go back to their homeland."

Swirl shrugged. "There's nothing to go back for. It's a dead land. Pollutants taint the soil. Nothing grows. It's a barren wasteland, home to the worst of wild beasts. Even the air is contaminated with the stench of death and rot."

The door opened and a young male centaur entered, carrying a tray. "We were hard-pressed to find something a human would want," he remarked. "But Belouth said everyone likes grains."

Swirl slipped a muscular arm around her, helping her to a sitting position. The grains turned out to be a large bowl of porridge studded with red berries, and after the first tentative bite, Ember devoured it.

"We'll send a message to the Sands to collect you at the border. But you must rest for at least a couple of days first. No point you dying of blood loss on the way."

He addressed the young centaur, "Guards on the door, with a message from me. Anyone coming near will wish they had not." Before Ember could ask, he continued, "Your presence has divided the camp. Some wish to kill you. But the centaurs you released from the Swords' dungeons speak in your favour, and so do I."

"Thank you." Although she trusted Swirl, her nerves increased markedly at the mention of those in the camp wishing her harm, and she wished she had her dagger with her. It wasn't in her belt and she had to assume it had been destroyed along with everything else she owned.

The young centaur gathered up her bowl and tray and opened the door. A flash of bright red flew past his ear and he started, almost spilling the bowl on the ground. With a quick word of apology, he left.

Ember's eyes widened accusingly. "Is that my firebird?"

The red bird landed on Swirl's back in a shower of sparks, preening himself. He jerked his head up, startled, as she spoke, and then, to Ember's amusement, looked completely abashed, and tried to hide his head under his wing.

"I can see you, you know," Ember told the bird with mock severity. "You were supposed to be back months ago!"

Swirl twitched a flank, and the bird wobbled and gave an aggrieved squawk, trying to regain his balance. "To be fair, you left the Swords. How was he supposed to know where to go?"

"Did he even try?"

"Well, no," the centaur admitted with a sly smile. "He got rather attached to life in the grasslands."

"To you, you mean," Ember said, as the bird hopped onto Swirl's shoulder and rubbed its beak affectionately against Swirl's cheek.

"He's a sweet thing," Swirl allowed, stroking the bird with a gentle finger.

Ember grinned. It was funny to see the huge, muscled centaur cooing over a small bird. She sank back onto the stretcher, wincing.

"Rest now," Swirl said. "You can attend to your bodily needs behind that panel. If you need anything, just call. There'll be a guard at your door, day and night."

"Thank you." She couldn't resist a yawn. Just the act of sitting and eating had stolen what little energy she had. When the door gently closed behind Swirl and the firebird, she closed her eyes and slept.

Chapter 13

E mber ended up staying in the camp for nearly a week. Although the Stones had received Swirl's message, they didn't appear in any hurry to get her and had requested she make her way to the border in a week's time. She was sulky at that, imagining them at dances and feasts, enjoying the lavish hospitality of the Sands in their magnificent castle.

By contrast, the camp in the grasslands was a decidedly rough affair. There were a few huts, and lots of gardens laid out in oddly curving shapes. The centaurs lived a nomadic life. Camps were temporary, established for only as long as resources held out before the herd moved on for better grazing, leaving their gardens to overgrow and reseed themselves, to become lush and fruitful on their return months later. This camp was just one of many.

Swirl was a chiron, a leader of the herd, but there were many herds and many leaders. Under normal circumstances, it would be difficult to unite them on any issue, but with the prospect of war looming, the centaurs were undivided. Defence of their land and their people was their only focus, and every day they trained, thundering up and down races marked out on the fields, and competing with their weapons:

bows, spears, slingshots, clubs, swords and battle axes. Even the children competed as soon as they were big enough to hold a spear, for as Swirl said, they might have to save their own lives one day.

Ember didn't venture far from her hut on the first day, but the next day, a company of female centaurs bore her away from the main camp's action, to their own more relaxing environs further away. The females didn't mix with the males except during the breeding season, but they trained just as hard as the males did.

Ember helped with the babies as much as her shoulder would allow, for she found them utterly engaging and very sweet, although they didn't seem to know how strong they were, and she gathered more than a few bruises on her shins from them accidentally kicking her. There was a plan to spirit the young ones away when the enemy came, but they didn't share any details with Ember, and she didn't blame them. Mostly she acted as a babysitter, calling for a herd mother if one of the babies strayed too far, and watching over them while they slept, all tangled up together in a pile of limbs and hooves.

She'd only caught sight of Rohane—the centaur who had shot her—once, and he'd given her such a contemptuous glare that she immediately pretended she hadn't seen him, and walked off in the opposite direction. Part of her wished she had his arrow as a souvenir, but it had been destroyed, along with everything else.

In the evenings, she returned to the main camp for a solitary meal. The guards didn't mind if she sat outside her hut, and she would eat to the sound of chanting, which Swirl said the centaurs did every evening as part of their forecasting rituals. The words sounded otherworldly and mysterious to Ember, and she liked the cadence, the way the sound rose and fell through the twilight air. When she closed her eyes, she felt as though the words were transporting her through galaxies of stars, spinning through space and time, and she would open her eyes with a gasp, the weight of gravity in the present bringing her back to her senses with a thud.

Although the ragged wound in her shoulder had been carefully stitched and poulticed with herbs by the centaur healers, it was going to be a long, slow road to recovery. One morning, when it was aching particularly badly, she asked Swirl about it, for the centaurs who had worked in the healing clinics of the Kingdom of Swords knew of the fae's magical healing balms and how to replicate them, but Swirl shook his head.

"What is of fae, isn't of us," he said simply.

"But if the fae are wounded, it'll only be minutes before they're ready to fight again. Surely you could make exceptions to keep the balance?"

Swirl smiled. "We only have to kill them once. Besides, we have other ways of healing."

"Then why aren't you using them on me?" Ember grumbled.

The smile left Swirl's face and his features grew dark and clouded. "You owe your life to Belouth, but as you've already saved his, your debt is cancelled. We do not want you further in our debt by owing us our medical skills."

Ember said no more, discomforted by his harsh tone, and Swirl left her, his tail twitching irritably. But he returned that evening with an apology and a handful of herbs soaked in fragrant oil. Under his instruction, she applied it to the pad covering her wound, and as the oil soaked through, the pain lessened considerably.

"We can't share all our secrets." His tone was gentle.

"I wouldn't tell. You know I wouldn't."

Swirl shrugged. "I can't foretell what you will do. I suppose that's humanity. Unpredictable." He changed the subject, saying, "The Stones will meet you at the border tomorrow. Be ready for an early start. We'll say our farewells now. I'll not have you waking me up."

His smile belied his terse words as he gave her a warm hug, urging her to be safe.

It was still dark when Belouth woke her, and on leaving the hut, she found to her dismay Rohane was with the group chosen to escort her. They had brought her a donkey for her to ride, small yet sturdy, for she'd been half afraid it wouldn't be big enough to carry her weight. But it bore her easily enough, and she followed the centaurs through the camping grounds, attracting sniggers and amused comments as she went.

"Couldn't we have gone round the long way?" she muttered, half to herself.

Rohane, a few paces ahead, replied with acerbity, "We want them to know you've actually gone," and Ember fell silent, wondering if all the centaurs had such good hearing or if it was just him.

They kept a walking pace for most of the day, and although Ember was grateful to ride, her legs and bottom became numb and then painfully sore. The donkey was saddled with a leather cloth topped with a thin cushion, and the bony back was uncomfortable. After a couple of hours, she was squirming, thankful when Rohane called a halt and she could slither off.

They had a bite to eat—the same porridge stuff she'd been eating all week, and a canteen of a sour milk drink, rather like thin yoghurt, both filling and refreshing. For the first time, perched on the side of a windswept hill, the beauty of the Free Grasslands was laid out before her.

The pastures spread as far as the eye could see, an undulating coverlet of green and brown, broken by the occasional clump of dark trees. Belouth pointed out their camp, but Ember was hard-pressed to see it. The conical roofs of the huts and the oddly shaped gardens blended in so cleverly to the environment, they were barely discernible. She wondered how many other camps were there, invisible to the naked eye, how many centaurs were training for the battles ahead. Hundreds, she supposed. Thousands.

The respite was brief and then they were on their way again, Ember gritting her teeth as the donkey plodded along. After an hour, she slid down to give her backside a break, but walking didn't last long. Her shoulder throbbed in painful bursts, and soon she was back on the donkey's back, wondering miserably how far the border was, but trying not to show how glum she felt. The centaurs were kind to accompany her, and she didn't want to rouse their ire by complaining. If they just dumped her here and left her to it, she'd fare much worse than previously, when she'd been roaming about on her own. Her injury had clouded that part of her mind that could charm anything, and she could barely sustain a partial camouflage for longer than five minutes.

To pass the time, she tried making conversation with her escort, but none were particularly forthcoming apart from Belouth, who recounted his story of his journey from the Kingdom of Swords, a dangerous journey at the best of times, but particularly harrowing when most of the company were ill, injured, and mentally fragile. They lost five on the way, and all required intensive care once they had reached the herds in the grasslands. Once they had crossed the border, Rohane told her solemnly, one of the elders simply keeled over and died. It was only the anticipation of seeing his home that kept him going for so long. Ember had tears in her eyes at that.

"But if it weren't for you," Rohane reassured her, "He would never have seen the sun set over his lands ever again. And neither would I."

He clasped her hand, and she had squeezed his in return. And then they turned to talking about Ember's own travels, and he gave her some foraging tips to increase the chances of survival out in the wilds. He showed her a plant she had seen often, with buds that looked like small balloons, and demonstrated how to bite the seam at the back of the pod to release a mouthful of pure water stored from previous rainstorms. He also pulled up a plant that seemed to grow everywhere. It had tiny leaves above ground, but extraordinarily thick roots, and once peeled, they revealed sweet flesh reminiscent of a banana.

It was nearing evening by the time they reached the border marked by a line of weathered, craggy rocks several metres apart, stretching off into the distance. Beyond, at the base of the scrub-covered hills leading to the deserts of the Sands, was another marker—clearly fae-made, for it was more a statue than a rock—carved into a large teardrop shape, glowing with a lustrous gleam in the hill's shadow.

The centaurs halted at the border, and Ember eased herself off the saddle with a groan of relief. All the centaurs had drawn their bows and arrows and were scanning the hills, alert and watchful. They waited, and just as Ember was about to say, "Well, where are they?" there came a familiar screech that echoed throughout the hills.

Dragon.

The donkey gave a squeal of dismay, tore its reins out of Ember's hands, pivoted and ran, and a few of the centaurs shifted their weight nervously from hoof to hoof as if keen to follow.

The dragons came into view, landing atop the hill as if in formation for a battle charge. She waved at them, and one dragon swooped down the hill, gliding to land just beyond the fae marker. She waited, but the rider didn't dismount. At that distance, she couldn't even see who it was, although it was clear the large green dragon was neither Lakin nor Beni.

"I'd better go, then," she said, when it became clear that the dragon-rider wasn't prepared to go any closer. "Thank you."

Belouth hugged her gently, mindful of her shoulder, and she nodded around to the others, Rohane raising a derisive eyebrow in acknowledgement.

Stepping beyond the marker was a surprise in itself. She had travelled along the border on Diamond's back, and had been aware of its sepia tone and the way it slowed the dragons' wings, but now she was on foot, details leapt out at her. The temperature had dropped. The birdsong and wind passing through the grasses that she'd taken for granted had stopped. Her footsteps were muffled, and she was suddenly conscious of her heartbeat thrumming in her ears, the rasping of her breath in and out of her lungs. It took a long time to cross the short distance, and her head seemed on a swivel, glancing this way and that as if crossing a busy road. This strip of land felt dangerous, wild, dystopian. It felt like an hour but was only minutes when she finally reached the other side, the colours, sounds and scents of the outdoors coming back in a rush as soon as she stepped over the invisible line into the Sands territory.

She recognised the dragon-rider as one of Sten's lesser advisors and tried not to feel insulted at that. There was no point putting the One and Two or the senior council members at risk, with several armed centaurs a few metres away. An arrow could reach them faster than a dragon could retaliate.

She waved farewell to the centaurs, and they leisurely turned and walked away, as though there was no need to gallop.

The advisor slipped off his mount's back and gave her a shallow bow, which she returned with difficulty, for all her muscles were aching. A look of concern crossed his face as he noticed the bandage peeking out from under her tunic.

"It was an accident. Sort of," she assured him.

Without a word, he retrieved a vial of healing balm from the panniers. She loosened the bandage, and he sprinkled her wound with a few drops. An icy sensation raced through her veins, chasing the pain away, the wound already knitting together.

He helped her onto the dragon, and she clutched the handholds at the sides, grateful that she could do so without the tremendous shooting pains she'd almost grown used to over the past week. The dragon launched itself into the air, and they were on their way, flying back with the fleet to the Kingdom of Stones.

CHAPTER 14

There was no break for food this time, and the dragons' strength and speed seemed to increase the closer the snowy peaks grew. As soon as they arrived, she was told to go straight to the throne room. Still travel-stained and windblown, she was abashed to find it full of advisors and upper courtiers. They fell silent as a guard escorted her through the crowd toward the dais, and she could feel the weight of their stares. A hand brushed hers as she passed, and she glanced back to see Kalin, who looked both relieved and furious in equal measure. Dragging her gaze away, she focused on the king and queen instead. Ruby appeared as regal as ever, but Sten was clearly showing the effects of several days' worth of carousing, his eyes bleary, cheeks flushed.

"Ember," Sten said. "We are pleased you are well."

Ember bowed. "Thank you, Your Majesty."

"What befell Diamond?" Ruby asked abruptly.

"The Seeds shot her," Ember said, and a rumble of consternation sounded throughout the hall.

"The Seeds have no weapons with which to defeat a dragon," Ruby said. "Much less a simple arrow."

"It was coated with poison which rotted her scales and did something to her blood. Made it bubble." She raised her voice to be heard over the outraged hum. "That wasn't what killed her, though. A garakworm attacked us."

"But *you* got away?"

Ruby's tone was almost accusatory, and Ember flushed. "I cast a barrier and smashed the worm with it. It disappeared."

There was another stir of talking, and Ruby raised her hand for silence. "We shall have a memorial for Diamond in the lower garden." She turned her attention back to Ember. "And then the centaurs rescued you?"

"Eventually," she said, not wanting to go into her experiences with the Seeds with so many eyes upon her. She could elaborate on that later, in private.

"But they shot you?"

"It was an accident. They thought I was a trespasser. But they helped me. They looked after me."

There came another stir of comment, and Sten said, "Then you'll be pleased to hear that we persuaded the Sands to remain apart from the Seeds' plotting. Whatever mischief that may make will be due to the Seeds alone. And the Swords," he added as an afterthought.

"Will the Seeds and Swords alone be enough to overturn the covenant of the grasslands?"

Sten and Ruby exchanged a glance. "It would depend on how much they want it," Sten observed, and Ember felt a chill crawl down her back. If Serafina was determined to take the grasslands, she would drive her armies into the ground before she let the centaurs win.

"You may go," Ruby said, waving a hand in dismissal. Ember bowed again, and retreated from the room, the chatter starting up again as the doors closed behind her. Ruby had seemed so aloof, so stern. Ember had always considered her a friend. Perhaps not.

She started off down the hallway back to her chambers, but she hadn't gone more than a few paces when the throne room door opened, and in a few strides, Kalin was at her side.

Formally, he went down on one knee before her, taking her hand in his. "My lady."

She looked at his bowed head, not really knowing what to do. Kalin was a high courtier, and she'd never seen him on bended knee to anyone. Finally, she said, "Please get up. I don't think our queen would like to see you on your knees to me."

He slowly rose and enfolded her in his arms. "When I heard Diamond had been shot ..." his arms tightened, and she felt the brush of his lips against her hair. "I truly felt as though my heart had been torn from my chest. Oh, Ember!"

She closed her eyes, liking the feel of his muscular arms around her, and slowly her arms went up around his neck, drawing him close. She turned her face up to his, meaning to tell him she had missed him too, and that she was glad to be home, but his lips found hers, preventing any words. Her response came automatically, because she enjoyed kissing and she liked Kalin, and the feeling of safety his presence aroused was comforting. She had been alone in the wilderness with danger and hunger lurking at every corner, and now she was safe in the palace, kissing a handsome fae who was clearly enthralled with her.

Her heart beat faster, and she opened her mouth to him, feeling the urgent press of his body against her. His hands were in her hair, and he was whispering against her mouth, "I must have you now, Ember, please say yes," and without really knowing what she was doing, she took his hand and led him down the corridors.

They were silent as they walked toward her chamber. She peeked up at him and he was practically bouncing on the balls of his feet, a broad grin of satisfaction across his face, but with every step she took, she felt a sensation of cold chasing away the warmth she had felt in his arms.

When they were at her chamber door, she almost didn't want to open it, but he kissed her again, unable to wait, and she felt herself pressed up against the door, unable to get away. He was gradually wringing a response from her that wasn't as eager as it might have been, but he seemed too caught up in the moment to care. And she liked the reminder that he was stronger than her, that he could easily overpower her through brute strength or magical means. It made her feel helpless, submissive, and she liked that feeling. She'd had to make decision after decision when she was fending for her life in the wild, and she didn't want to make decisions anymore. She wanted to be led. She wanted to be taken.

"Open the door, Ember," Kalin said. His blue eyes were glittering with lust, his breathing ragged, and she obeyed him.

He swept her up into his arms and in four strides was across the room, and laying her on the bed. And now the tone changed. Where before he had been the forceful, he was now almost polite, timid. He crawled onto the bed with her and kissed her again. She wanted him to rip her clothes off and have her, but she didn't quite know how to tell him, and so she kissed him fiercely, placing his hands on her breasts, but he didn't seem to get the message.

"Take it off," she eventually commanded, and he eagerly pushed the fabric away from her shoulders, but almost at once checked himself, taking in the sunburst scar the arrow had wrought.

"My lady! They said you'd been shot, but ..." he reached out to trace the knotted flesh and then withdrew his hand as if scared to touch it.

"The centaurs didn't want to use fae magic, so it took a week or so before I could get some healing balm."

"If they'd done it earlier, there wouldn't be a scar."

"I don't mind it." She quite liked it, actually. It looked dangerous, fierce, as though she'd overcome something terrible, which, in a way, she had. Another battle scar to add to the list, she thought, only this one was visible.

She reached for Kalin again and he kissed her gently, but the mood was broken, and suddenly she found his soft touch irritating.

"Kalin," she said, pulling him closer. "I'm not going to break."

She bit his neck, harder than she intended, and felt the breath hiss out from him. She slid her hands down to his cock and found it hard and wanting. She stroked it through his pants and then undid the ties on his tunic. He pulled it off, leaving him bare-chested, and she licked one of his nipples, and then sucked and bit it while he groaned with pleasure. It was she who was the aggressor now, sitting astride him and rubbing herself against the jutting length still encased in his pants. Just the feel of it was enough to send a shiver through her, and she closed her eyes for a moment, imagining she was astride someone with eyes like burning coals, whose hands and mouth would be all over her now, squeezing and groping until she cried out in pain and pleasure.

The thought made the blood thrum in her veins and she quickly pulled her top off and unclipped the band the Stones typically used to encase the breasts—no lacy trim here. She caressed her breasts and pinched her nipples as she rocked back and forth, and still he didn't touch her, just lay back against the pillows, his eyes wide, drinking her all in.

It made her want to slap him.

Instead, she got off him and went to the bathroom.

"Ember?" he called.

"Just wait," she said, and closed the door.

She looked at herself in the mirror. Her hair was tousled, her pupils dilated, her cheeks flushed. Was she really going to do this with him? She took a quick shower, washing off the day's travels, and when she went back to the room, she still hadn't decided.

He was lying under the sheets now, his clothes piled neatly on the floor, and when she let the towel drop, the sheet covering his groin stirred. Slowly she came closer, and slipped onto the bed, pulling the sheet down to see him. His cock swelled under her gaze and that decided her. It would be a shame to waste it, she thought, and slid astride him, his cock resting against her arse. She leaned over him, teasing his mouth with her breasts.

He kissed them gently, and she sighed with irritation.

"Harder," she said, and he did, drawing a nipple into his mouth, his tongue laving her. "Harder." He sucked hard enough to make her moan, and she rocked, rubbing her clit against his groin, using his body to pleasure herself with no thought of pleasing him. It felt good. Without breaking eye-contact, she inched up his body until she was poised over his face.

"Lick me," she said, and holding onto the carved headboard for balance, lowered down onto his mouth.

He obeyed immediately, his tongue and lips working against her, a slick hot friction that made her gasp and wriggle, to get into a better position.

"Play with my arse," she gasped, and then his hands were squeezing and slapping her rump. A finger slowly slid inside her anus, and she moaned, spreading her legs wider to give him better access.

She looked back over her shoulder and his cock was rigid, but she didn't care. Instead, she focused on her own pleasure, darts of fire spreading up through her, and then finally, a hot release that had her clenching her thighs against him, as she rode his mouth, crying out incoherently. Finally, when her legs had stopped trembling, she eased herself off him.

"Thank you," she said. She reached for his shirt and wiped his mouth. He was breathing hard, his pupils dilated, and she slowly eased her thumb into his mouth, smiling when he moaned and sucked on it.

"Touch yourself," she said, and watched dispassionately as he took hold of his cock, pumping it. It swelled even more under his hand, and he groaned.

"Harder," she said. "Faster."

Again, he obeyed, and just to see what he'd do, she slowly licked her lips and bent to his cock as though she was about to enclose it in her mouth, and stopped short.

"Please," he said, and his voice sounded like a whimper. "Please, Ember."

His helpless yearning for her was driving another need within her. She enjoyed seeing him like this.

"Don't come," she warned him, and then she took his hands, forcing them down at his sides. He was taller and stronger than her. He could have easily resisted, but he didn't. Still holding his wrists, she took him in her mouth, sucking and licking him, swallowing him down as far as she could, faster and faster, until he was groaning and thrusting his hips up to meet her.

Resisting him, she sat up, and in one fluid motion, slid onto his erect cock. He arched his back as her wet heat enclosed his rock hard length, and his hands gripped her thighs,.

"Don't come," she repeated, panting a little, for it felt soooo good. She slid her hands down her body, watching the way he watched her, unable to take her eyes off her, and then slipped two fingers down to her clit. She rubbed and stroked herself, and he restlessly thrust against her, wanting some of that friction for himself.

"Don't fucking move," she said crossly, and eased herself off his cock in warning.

He groaned in desperation and whimpered, "no, please," and she slowly sank back down again.

Again, she played with herself, and then she began to rock, ever so slowly. His eyes were closed, and his legs were trembling with the effort of restraint. That made her feel even more powerful. She stroked his nipples as she kissed his neck, and he groaned aloud.

"Fuck, Ember, you make me crazy, you know that? You're so wet, so delicious ..."

"Shut up," she said.

With a flash of resentment, he thrust upward, tried to grasp her hips, and she slapped his hands away, and then slapped him, hard, across his face. She felt the jerk of his cock inside her, heard the moan of pain mingled with pleasure, and as he fell back onto the rumpled sheets, she knew he liked it, that he was just as submissive as she liked to be.

"Naughty," she warned. "Apologise."

"I'm sorry, my lady," he groaned, and his face was suffused with unadulterated adoration, smeared with the sexual bliss of finding someone who understood him, and would treat him the way he needed to be treated. He was a high courtier, with endless responsibilities, and the power of life and death over others. He needed someone to be in charge of him. She wasn't just his lady, she realised. She was his queen.

And yet, he wasn't what she wanted, not really, but she had no one else, and so she rode him, hard, until he was crying out her name, and when she had taken her own satisfaction, she said, "You can come now," and he did, in a shaking rush.

She eased herself off him and waited until he had come back to himself. He looked as though he was about to go to sleep, and she knew it was mean, but she didn't want him sleeping in her bed.

"You better go," she said, gently. "I'm tired."

He blinked at her and slowly sat up. He reached for her, but she adroitly slid away, picking up the damp towel and wrapping it around her.

"I'll see you at training tomorrow."

"Of course."

Once he had dressed, he went to the door, looking half-dazed as though he wasn't quite sure how he had got there or what had just happened. He looked back at her as if expecting her to call him back, but she just smiled at him.

"See you later."

He smiled uneasily and left, closing the door quietly behind him. Once she was alone, she sank back down onto her bed. The physical release hadn't satisfied her as much as she thought it might, and she had a feeling that she'd made a terrible mistake. She was tired, but she didn't really want to sleep in the bed anymore. Instead, she nestled into the soft couch and fell asleep, tears oozing slowly down her cheeks.

CHAPTER 15

Ember trudged down the snowy pathways toward the lower garden with the rest of the court, her hood wrapped tightly about her face as protection from the numbing chill of the morning. She, like everyone else, was in a sombre mood, and there was scarcely any chatter as they walked.

The palace fae arranged themselves along the terraces of the garden basin, and Ember found herself next to Apoli, the vivacious niece of the queen. Apoli's hands were boldly tucked into a glossy grey sealskin muff, which she said she'd bought in one of the nearby villages, but everyone knew it had been sent to her from an admirer from the Skies, sealskin being somewhat rare high in the mountains. Ember was surprised by Apoli's audacity. A foreigner had murdered one of their dragons, and she wouldn't have thought it wise to wear something from another kingdom at the memorial, but Apoli didn't seem to care.

She was also surprised to see Diamond's body displayed on a flat slab of rock in the centre of the garden basin, her wounds disguised with garlands of white snowdaisies. The flowers grew all over the mountains, poking their tenacious little heads up through untouched snowdrifts. Snowdaisies were a symbol of the Stones, a reminder of their ability to thrive and adapt in the harshest of conditions.

"How did Diamond get here?" she whispered to Apoli. "I thought she'd disappeared forever."

"She returned home to us," Apoli whispered back, her eyes glistening with tears. "They always do."

Glancing around, she caught sight of Kalin gazing at her from the other side of the garden. Ever since their tryst, he had been sending little gifts, hovering close, patiently waiting for her to acknowledge him, and she found it irritating. It wasn't so much his manner, as the knowledge it was she who had provoked and encouraged him in the first place. After that first awkward training session, when he'd done everything but lick her hand like an excited puppy, she'd cried off training with him and spent time in her room instead, keeping herself busy with painting a gift for Sten and Ruby, and practising casting glamours without the brush Alena had once given her, now lost on a hill somewhere.

Kalin hadn't protested, had made no attempt to change her mind, or force her to train with him. He had merely accepted her decision with a practised courtier's smile and a promise that should she wish to resume her training, he would be glad to help. Now, at every public meeting or court dinner, his eyes were on her, ever watchful, ever hopeful, and every few days she found a posy or a beautifully written love poem at her chamber door.

"You mistreat him, you know," Apoli said.

"What?" Ember said, startled. It was as though Apoli had read her mind.

"He's infatuated with you. You shouldn't have had sex with him if you didn't feel the same way."

Ember gave a startled laugh. "Apoli, you have sex with everyone." It was true. Courtiers, guards, servants, male, female, a single fae or several at one time, Apoli, like most of the fae, loved to enjoy herself.

"Yes, but everyone I have sex with knows it's just for fun. Kalin thought it was for love." She frowned at Ember. "You should have told him it wasn't. And besides," her eyes flashed with envy, "I hear humans have some special kind of sex magic. You shouldn't have used it on him."

Ember frowned. "I don't think I did."

It was true. She and Cole had been consumed with each other. He was obsessed with her, a glutton for her, and she had gladly participated, not even caring her mind was wasting away. Ashe was much more controlled than Cole, disciplined and aloof, and even he had given in to his base urges, and she had encouraged him, longing for his touch. Desperate even now, if she thought about it.

Kalin wasn't pounding on her door demanding her favour. And she wasn't bereft at his absence, yearning to be in his arms, desperate to have pleasure wrung from her, drop by excruciating drop.. He was just infatuated and it would pass; she was sure of it.

"You should tell him. He thinks you will call for him and then you will live together like happy little pigs in a pen, and have strange little human-fae babies who can't even mould stone."

Ember laughed at the thought of it. Having fae offspring wasn't a simple matter of sperm meets egg. There was a whole ritual attached to it, for which Ember was fervently grateful. Imagine if Cole had got her pregnant! The very idea sent a chill down her back. And then she wondered what it would be like to have a baby with dark eyes and colours blooming like oil on water under brown skin, and she felt a tenderness in her belly. She reached down to touch it, before whipping her hand away, pretending she only had an itch.

"Or perhaps you should." There was a wistful note in Apoli's voice which surprised Ember. She'd never thought of Apoli as the maternal type. "Kalin would be a good father, a true soulmate. And I think he would make very handsome babies."

Ember shook her head emphatically. "Maybe for someone else."

Apoli gave a sideways glance at Kalin and her expression grew soft. Ember was about to remark on that, but a loud screech interrupted her. Both shielded their eyes, gazing up into the bright white glare of the sky, looking for the black dot they knew was coming closer and closer.

"There," Apoli nudged Ember, pointing, and a massive yellow dragon plummeted out of the sky, landing with an earth-shaking thud on the empty concourse of the basin.

"Gemstar!" cried the familiar voice of the Stone mage, his sonorous tones magically echoing throughout the terraces. Everyone clapped, Ember belatedly joining in. She craned her neck for a glimpse of the mage standing next to Sten and Ruby at the apex of the basin. He was as underdressed as ever, clad only in his thin grey robes while everyone else was bundled up warmly in furs and fleece, but the cold didn't appear to bother him.

The dragon lowered his head and screeched again, and Ember had to resist the urge to clap her hands to her ears. He rose on his hind legs, arched his neck and blasted a ball of fire at Diamond, blistering her flesh. And then he leapt forward and bit Diamond's head off.

Ember gasped with horror, her hand covering her mouth in dismay as Gemstone crunched down, Diamond's skull splitting under massive teeth, the splintering of bone echoing around the basin.

A tear rolled down Apoli's smooth cheek. "So young. So sad," she whispered.

There came another screech from somewhere overhead and a clamorous thud as another dragon hit the dirt, and the Stone mage called "Brimstone!" to a surge of applause.

The new dragon flapped his green wings with a clap of percussion before baring his teeth in a snarl. He seized Diamond's leg and ripped it off, gnawing on it like a dog with a bone. He shook it, and shreds of flesh came away, scattering across the concourse.

Another dragon arrived — "Garland!" — and Gemstone, having devoured Diamond's entire head, took to the air, swooping low over the watching crowd before flying off into the mountains.

On and on it went, with dragons arriving, screeching their welcome (or commiseration, Ember wasn't quite sure), and then ripping Diamond's body apart until there was nothing left but a few burned bones. The last dragon to arrive was very old, so ancient that she had barely any teeth, her wings ragged, her muzzle blackened with age. She shuffled around, gnawing the charred bones, and licking up smears of blood, until the concourse was as clean as if nothing had happened at all. The fae applauded, and she took to the skies with much groaning and creaking of limbs, like an old lady easing herself out of her rocking chair.

When she had gone, it appeared the ceremony was over too. There were no speeches or singing or anything that Ember associated with funeral or memorial services. The fae simply filed out of the lower garden and returned to the palace and surrounding dwellings, murmuring to each other in low voices, clouds of steam hanging over their heads in the frosty air.

"That was ... interesting," she said to Apoli, as they walked through the garden, their boots crunching along the snow-covered paths.

"I knew you were going to say something foreign and odd," Apoli crowed. "You had no clue, did you?"

"Clearly not," Ember said, slightly nettled. She and Apoli had been friends from the first time she'd visited the Kingdom of Stones, but ever since the business with Kalin, Apoli's tongue had become rather sharp. And although Ember knew she probably deserved it, she still didn't like it very much.

"Diamond's dragon magic flows through her veins, even after death," Apoli explained. "And the others absorb it. That last one, Hymernes, is ancient. Death stands at her shoulder, but Diamond's blood and bones will give her strength to carry on for years yet."

"Do all the dragons get memorials at the palace?"

"Oh no. Diamond only did because she served the crown. Usually, the dragons die far out in the mountains. They have their own rituals, but I'm told it's much like this." She left Ember inside the palace with a kiss on her cheek as if in apology for her former brusqueness, and somewhat mollified, Ember returned to her chamber.

She peeled off her outerwear, sent her servant for something warm to drink, and then studied the canvas she'd been working on, her lips pursed in concentration.

It was a picture of Diamond riding the wind, her wings outstretched, neck proudly arched, a blast of fire erupting from her mouth. She'd got all the details right: the jagged yellow markings down the side of her neck, the humourous look in her eye as though she were laughing at a private joke.

"Lovely Diamond," she murmured.

"You'd like some diamonds, my lady?" said the servant, who had returned to the room with Ember's hot spiced drink, so quietly that Ember hadn't heard her enter. "Some jewellery?"

Amused, Ember explained what she meant, and asked the servant to request an audience with the One and Two. She sipped her drink, and then, still feeling chilly, had a hot bath and changed into an outfit that was a little more formal than what she usually wore: a fitted tunic with flowing pants in green, and emerald studded pins in her hair.

When the reply finally came, she lugged her painting down the hallways until she got to Sten and Ruby's private chambers. The sitting room was warm and cosy with a fire crackling. Sten was ensconced in an armchair with a mug of cider while Ruby reclined gracefully on a low-backed chaise. She had an embroidered handkerchief in her hand and her eyes were red; she'd been crying, Ember guessed.

Ember bowed somewhat clumsily, with her arm wrapped around her painting. "Good afternoon, Your Majesties."

Ruby gave a wan smile. "It's always upsetting when one of the family dies. Wasn't it a beautiful memorial? The weather was kind."

"It was very ..." Ember flailed for the right word. "Moving."

"Just so, just so," Sten gestured at the picture. "What have you there?"

"A gift, Your Majesty. I painted Diamond for you."

She turned the painting about to face them, a little shyly, for she always found it hard letting others judge her work.

Sten and Ruby looked at it. Ruby's mouth sagged and Sten tilted his head.

"It's very ..." Ruby said faintly, in much the same way as Ember had just moments earlier when describing Diamond's memorial. "You must have put a lot of effort into it."

"Diamond?" said Sten, a hint of incredulity in his voice. "Are you sure?"

Ember's cheeks burned, but she tried not to feel offended. The fae often found human art difficult to appreciate. Instead, using the power of a glamour she'd been practising, a glamour that her old friend Tasar had helped her with so long ago, she gently stroked Diamond from her head to her tail. Immediately, the painted dragon arched her back and let out an inaudible roar, before flying about the painted skies and landing on a snowy mountain peak.

"Yes!" Sten said in delight. "There she is!"

Ruby dabbed her eyes with her handkerchief. "Oh my. How lovely, Ember dear. Thank you."

Ember carefully leaned the painting against the wall. "I'm very sorry about what happened to Diamond."

"Now, now. It wasn't your fault." Sten looked over at Ruby for confirmation, but Ruby apparently hadn't heard him and had buried her face in her handkerchief. Ember was about to tell of her adventure in the Seeds jungle, but was interrupted by an urgent knock at the door, and a servant burst in without even waiting to be admitted.

"Your Majesties," he blurted, his face drained of colour. "Your attendance is required in the throne room at once. The Adjudicator has arrived."

CHAPTER 16

S ten and Ruby exchanged a wordless glance, but Ember could almost see the conversation flashing between them. Ruby rose gracefully, a hint of ice in her words. "Then let us not keep him waiting. Ember, you may go."

She waved a hand and her clothes transformed from the rather informal tunic and pants she had been wearing to purple robes encrusted with silver thread and jewels, a crown on top of her perfectly coiffed head. She had dressed Sten in similarly regal robes, and he nodded in thanks.

The pair swept past Ember as though they hadn't even seen her, and she quickly sank into a bow. It was the first time she had seen them formally dressed since her arrival as their guest, and she had forgotten how impressive they looked when they had a mind.

She waited a moment, and then, willing herself camouflaged, went after them.

They must have travelled by arcane means, for although she sprinted to the throne room, they were already seated, and she slipped through the great doors just as the guards were sealing it. A very pretty, very nervous servant escorted the Adjudicator to the dais—not that it mattered what she looked like, Ember thought. The Adjudicator had no need for pretty.

He was dressed as always in his red robes, his eyes blazing from behind his hood, and for once, he was alone without his ever-present entourage. Neither Ruby nor Sten bothered to rise to greet him and merely inclined their heads in acknowledgement. He didn't like that, Ember thought. He hated to be reminded he wasn't an actual ruler, although he was the oldest and most powerful in all of Esha.

She tiptoed along the wall, intending to hide herself behind some statuary at the side of the room just in case her disguise wore off. The Adjudicator turned just as she was ducking out of sight, and she froze, desperately hoping the porcelain dragon statue and her camouflage would be enough to escape his scrutiny. His gaze passed over her but didn't linger, and she let out a slow breath as he turned back to face the throne.

"You have visited the Sands." His voice was the scratching of winter boughs at a windowpane, disturbing, frigid.

"A little holiday," Ruby said lightly, and gestured toward the windows and the gentle snow falling outside. "It can get dreadfully dreary by the end of winter. How lucky for the Sands to enjoy summer all year round."

"Too hot," Sten said briefly. "And the sand gets everywhere."

"You had a lovely time!" Ruby chided. She turned to the Adjudicator. "He had spiced goat stew every morning for breakfast, and when we returned home, he harangued the cooks until they found a recipe for it. I keep telling him that a simple diet of grains and fruit would be much more suitable for someone of his age and … build, but he wasn't having any of it. Spiced goat stew every morning, and that lemon dish for dinner, what was it called? With the mint leaves on top?"

"Tenjaal," Sten said.

Ruby clapped her hands. "Tenjaal! Now that was an utter delight. And good for the figure, so I'm told."

She was prattling, and Ruby never prattled. She was worried, and trying to cover her worry with an air of lightness and frivolity, but the Adjudicator wasn't to be diverted.

"And what did you discuss with the rulers of the Sands over your … goat stew?"

Again, another one of those lightning conversations passed between the rulers.

Sten replied smoothly, "We discussed the peace of Esha and how to maintain it for the good of all the kingdoms." He inclined his head slightly and then raised an eyebrow, as if daring the Adjudicator to call him a liar.

The Adjudicator took up the dare. "I say you were deliberately colluding with a rival kingdom against the Seeds and the Swords to destabilise the country."

Sten's genial look disappeared, and his brows came together in a thick frown. The room darkened, and the snow falling outside became thicker, the flakes whirling past the windows. He was angry. Ember had never seen him angry before.

"Might I remind you where you are?" he said smoothly, and there came the low screech of a dragon outside somewhere. The Adjudicator flinched, ever so slightly, which gave Ember immense satisfaction. "My word is not to be doubted in my own palace."

"Your words are brave, Your Majesty, but I have the ear of all of Esha, and Esha tells me you are seeking support from another kingdom. Might I remind you who *I* am? I am the one who maintains balance. I keep the peace. And I say that you are treading on very dangerous ground."

Sten leapt to his feet, a forefinger pointing at the Adjudicator. "You have put a dead puppet on the Swords' throne. They have deliberately sought company with the Seeds in order to extend their territories claiming a free peoples' lands, and they do so at your bidding. You have deliberately thwarted tradition and I say you seek only that which you can have for yourself—"

His voice cut out as he clutched his throat, his face turning purple. He looked as though he was trying to tear away an invisible hand. Ruby went white, and she rose from her throne, but a force pushed her back. The dragon screech outside grew louder and then there came the thudding of a heavy body landing just outside the window, and another guttural roar which set the chandeliers rattling.

Sten fell to his knees. Ruby and the guards had been frozen by the Adjudicator's magic and could only watch their king with a helpless, bewildered impotence as he writhed on the dais.

Ember's own power was like a child's compared to the Adjudicator. There was no barrier she could create that would protect Sten for more than a nanosecond. But she could still move, and so she did, sliding one of the emerald pins from her hair, and hastening toward the Adjudicator on light, quick steps. She drove the sharp point into his withered hand, the only piece of flesh unconcealed by his robes.

He hissed with annoyance, snatching his hand away as a pinprick of blood welled, and the invisible force holding everyone in the room vanished. Ruby rose, so suffused with anger that red sparks were rising from her in an undulating wave. Sten rose too, suddenly appearing much larger than he had previously, and the guards as one slapped their hands to their sword hilts, the clank of steel echoing around the room. With a resounding crash, the window shattered, letting in a blast of frigid air and a whirling of snowflakes as Lakin forced its head through, heedless of glass shards still clinging to the frames. He roared with fury, belching forth a sheet of fire that scorched the floors black.

Ember was already scuttling backward, but the energy from the blast added to her momentum, and she hit the ground in a flailing heap. Her camouflage dropped for an instant before she quickly restored it, but to her chagrin, Ruby had noticed, her eyes widening, a frown creasing her brow. Scrambling back on her butt as fast as she could, Ember retreated to the doors and then got to her feet, ready to run.

The Adjudicator cast a barrier to protect himself with a flick of his hand. When all was still, he said with forced calm, "Keep your beast under control."

Sten shrugged with a casual air. "They do as they must, to keep the peace in our kingdom."

He stepped off the dais, and strolled over to Lakin, casually scratching him where most dragons liked best, between the horns. The dragon purred, but didn't take his eyes off the figure in the red cloak.

"There will be no travelling between kingdoms until further notice. The Swords, Seeds and Skies agree, and I shall speak with the Sands as soon as I am done here." The Adjudicator glanced with distaste at the scorched floors and the broken windows, as if silently questioning why anyone would bother themselves with coming to the Kingdom of Stones.

"The Skies have cloistered themselves from Esha matters ever since their last election," said Ruby. "And who can trust a Sword or a Seed to keep their word?"

"I shall keep it," said the Adjudicator. "And so will you."

Sten and Ruby gave shallow bows as if in agreement, but sparks still rose from Ruby in a cloud of pique, and Sten's fists were white at the knuckles. The Adjudicator vanished with a clap of air rushing to fill the empty space, and the dragon gave a smoky snort through his nostrils as if to say, "good riddance".

"Ember," said Ruby sternly. "Leave us. I'll speak with you later."

Sten reared back in surprise as Ember, utterly chagrined at being called out in front of everyone, let her camouflage drop, bobbed an awkward bow and hastily departed. The shame of being caught sneaking into their private audience with the Adjudicator! Sten would not be happy that she witnessed his shame at being strangled in his own throne room. He'd have some harsh words to say to her later, she was sure of it.

Ember let herself into her chamber and paced the floor, thinking hard. The threat of war had hung over their heads for months now, yet the Adjudicator was only prompted to take action when the Stones visited the Sands. The inference was the Adjudicator, far from being impartial, wanted the Swords and Seeds aligned to take over the grasslands without opposition. But she had seen the expressions of the One and Two. Both were furious about their treatment in front of the court. Although the Adjudicator had professed to want peace, he'd deliberately provoked a fight, and what, thought Ember, was the point of that?

CHAPTER 17

Far from being mollified by the Adjudicator's edict, and with her nerves jangling from the threat of the One and Two's displeasure, Ember abandoned her painting for training. Painting allowed her mind to run free, and she was tired of worrying about what the Adjudicator was up to, and when Ruby was going to shout at her. So, she spent the next few days in the training arenas instead, aiming for targets that seemed to move frustratingly a few inches to either side just as she released her arrows, and practising hand-to-hand sparring with the trainers.

Her sparring sessions weren't so much fist-fighting as wrestling, for the Stones were usually so padded up because of the inclement weather that a swung fist had little effect. But they had their own style of wrestling, *junko*, a sport which often inspired enormous wagers on the outcome. Every two years, the palace hosted a junko tournament that drew competitors from all over the kingdom, for the winner would earn enough to feed their village for an entire season.

Today, her trainer was teaching her how to take her opponent's weight and use it against them to throw them down, and they practised that move a few times, Ember finding it easier with each repetition. And then the trainer attacked using a move she'd only ever seen performed by others, lifting her off the ground from behind, her arms immobilised. She kicked back ineffectually at their shins, and the grip abruptly fell away. She stumbled as she tried to regain her balance, and whipped around to see Kalin with the trainer in a stranglehold. The trainer's face was steadily becoming the colour of a bruised berry.

"Let him go, Kalin!"

The trainer gave a strangled gasp, and Kalin's grip tightened, the veins standing out on his arm. His eyes were hard, his face contorted with anger. He showed no sign of relinquishing his hold and Ember shoved him. "Let him go, I said!"

He blinked and seemed to return to himself, relaxing his arm and letting the trainer loose. "My lady, I apologise, I thought —"

"Don't apologise to me," she said, incredulous. "You nearly strangled him!"

The trainer was on his knees, getting rather shakily to his feet. "Forgive me, my lady, my lord," he said, bowing to them both.

"You've got nothing to apologise for," Ember told him, and turned on Kalin. "You thought what? He was *teaching* me. He's a trainer. That's his *job*."

She was angrier than she should have been, but he had gone too far. She was sick of his pleading looks whenever they found themselves in the same room together; she was tired of the little notes and gifts he kept sending her, and she was fed up with him wanting more than she could ever give him.

"Enough. This stops now. Kalin, I can't be what you want me to be. I don't feel like that about you."

He looked utterly crushed. His face fell, and he tried to take her hand. "I apologise, Ember, but—"

"Not to me!" she said, gritting her teeth and snatching her hand away. "To him."

Kalin gave the trainer a terse nod, and the trainer scuttled back in a half-bow, his hand rubbing his throat.

"I love you, Ember."

"No, you don't. You don't know me. I'm sorry I led you on."

He frowned in confusion and she clarified, "I'm sorry for toying with your feelings. I want nothing more than to be friends."

His face became hard. "We shared a connection. I felt your spirit touch mine. We became one."

"No." She took his hand and his face brightened, and she hastily dropped it again. "No, you need someone nice. Someone who feels for you the same way you feel for me. I cannot love you the way you want, the way you deserve. I—"

She was about to say, "I love someone else," when a guard appeared.

He bowed low. "My lady, their majesties command your presence in the retiring room."

Her heart sank. "Oh."

"We can talk this through," Kalin said. "I shall see you afterwards."

"No," she replied gloomily, remembering Ruby's face when she had ordered Ember from the throne room. "You probably won't."

The guard escorted her to a small room, one of the many informal rooms the royals used to receive guests. The fireplace was empty, and the atmosphere was as chilly as the room. Sten and Ruby sat together on a high-backed couch without a hint of a smile, and Ember immediately sank into a bow.

"Sit," Sten said. With a sense of relief at being allowed to sit, rather than being forced to stand on the rug before them like a naughty schoolgirl, Ember took the chair opposite. "You showed a great deal of temerity, trespassing on our meeting uninvited."

Sten's voice was low and quiet, his disappointment palpable.

Ember looked down at her hands in her lap. "I apologise."

Ruby spoke. "If the Adjudicator had known you were there, he would have held us responsible for harbouring a fugitive, a thief. You put us all in danger."

Ember's head shot up at that. She hadn't even considered that possibility.

"I'm sorry." Her voice throbbed with sincerity. "I was curious about his visit. I wanted to know what he was going to say. I hate him," she finished viciously.

Sten's lips quirked in a grudging smile. "He is not well liked. His methods are ... humiliating." Almost unconsciously, his hand went up to touch his throat.

Ember flared up. "He had no right to do that. You were defending your kingdom, as is your right, and he has no—"

"Enough!" Ruby said sharply. "We have made many allowances for you, given your background. But we cannot allow you to speak to us like this. This is your only warning."

Ember wanted to apologise again, but she didn't dare. She bit her lip and nodded.

"He has overreached, and his behaviour shows he is angling for war," said Sten. "We have heard tales of Serafina's rule in the Swords. She has no decorum."

Ember didn't want to ask Sten to expand, but she found she was hungry for news of the Swords. It was her home for a long time. And hearing about Serafina was almost like hearing about Ashe. After all, she wore him around her neck.

As if reading her mind, Sten continued, "Lavish balls, each more luxurious and obnoxious than the last. Building of new halls, new extensions to the palace. Servants and courtiers missing, presumed dead. Public executions of those considered hostile to the crown. She is squandering resources, both money and fae. There are whispers of rebellions in the countryside and entire villages burned for insolence. The Kingdom of Swords is in disarray, and yet the Adjudicator lectures us about our behaviour. It's hypocritical."

The news was worse than Ember imagined. Images of smoke rising from the ashes of the pretty villages she had seen, fae hanging from rafters or butchered in the streets by armed guards, danced through her head. That would never have happened if Ashe had ruled, and somehow, she couldn't see it happening if Cole had worn the crown, either. He was vicious and volatile, but he wasn't stupid. He wouldn't have drained the kingdom's coffers for his own personal amusement.

She raised a tentative hand, as if she was in school, and Ruby inclined her head, indicating she might speak.

"Perhaps the Adjudicator is behind that too," she ventured. "Perhaps it suits him to have Serafina run mad."

Sten narrowed his eyes, nodding. "You may be right. Although why ...?" He shrugged. "It doesn't matter. The Two said you helped to attract the Adjudicator's attention away from me," and again his hand went to his throat, as if he couldn't quite believe that someone would dare to harm him.

"Which is the only reason we are showing leniency," said Ruby, her eyes glittering.

"I pricked him with my hairpin. And I'm not sorry," Ember added, just in case either of them thought she was going to apologise for it.

Sten guffawed and even Ruby smiled.

"A hairpin!" Sten said. "Let's arm our guards with them."

"I thought you might have cast one of your barriers. You're very good at them." Ruby may have thawed, but she still had a look of suspicion in her eye Ember couldn't quite decipher.

"They're the only thing I'm good at. I'm still having trouble with the rest."

Sten shrugged. "That will come. You need more lessons. I'll send Xarin to help you. He works with some of our —" he coughed. "Younger students."

Ember felt a flash of chagrin, knowing full well who Xarin was. He was practically the equivalent of a kindergarten teacher.

"You may go." Ruby said.

Ember rose to leave and bowed again. She was almost at the door when Sten spoke, his voice menacing.

"And, Ember ..."

She glanced back at him, and was brought up short. His face was suddenly more *fae* than she had ever seen it, his expression devoid of sympathy or empathy, his eyes empty, an almost bestial cast to his features. He held up a hand, and power crackled in a blue haze, coiling around his fingertips like a languorous snake. All at once, with a sinking heart, she was reminded he held her life in his hands. The kindness he had shown her thus far wasn't out of courtesy or friendship. It was because she amused him, because it suited him to have something he could hold over the Adjudicator and the Kingdom of Swords. She was just a pretty pawn here, her human life was worth nothing, and she was stupid to have forgotten her place.

"... don't ever presume on our hospitality again, or you'll be cast out to never again enjoy a warm welcome from the Kingdom of Stones."

Ember felt her cheeks grow hot, and her stomach churned with disquiet. "I am really very sorry. It was rude of me. I won't do it again."

"See that you don't," Ruby said, her stony expression a match for Sten's, her teeth glistening sharp and white. "Or we'll set the dragons on you."

Ember wasn't sure whether to smile at that, but neither showed any hint of humour, and she swallowed, bowed, and scuttled from the room.

Chapter 18

Every morning at dawn, depending on the weather, Ember jogged around the grounds or through the palace hallways. The guards grew used to seeing her huffing and puffing around the corridors and ignored her, after a few initial instances of them drawing their weapons and demanding to know who was chasing her. After breakfast, she practised archery and junko throws until her limbs were shaking. She had something to eat and a brief break, and then trained with a spear, jabbing at straw filled bags, and practising the twirling motions that characterised the Stone's attack and defence motions.

For all the Adjudicator's posturing that kingdoms weren't to fraternise, she wanted to be prepared if war ever came to the mountains. And how would war affect Earth? She knew the fortunes of the fae affected humankind. A simple change in the ruling of the Swords had increased temperatures on Earth, while strife with the Seeds was likely to increase the incidence of pestilence and disease, and if the Stones got involved, Earth could expect normally sound governments to topple or succumb to corruption.

She learned fairly quickly that the Stones' guards didn't take their training as seriously as those in the Kingdom of Swords. The Stones' mountains were a formidable barrier for any army to negotiate, and, of course, they had the reputation and strength of their dragons behind them. Still, the guards were more skilled than Ember, and there was always something new to learn from them.

In the afternoons, when her body was too weary to continue, she practised her charms with Xarin, who proved a patient tutor. It was a wonderful day when she finally learned how to make a groove in a rock with her finger, and she presented it to Apoli with the air of a child presenting a parent with a crayoned artwork. However, unlike a doting parent, Apoli immediately burst into gales of laughter, and took it to show her friends, so they could laugh at her too, which was galling.

Kalin kept his distance from her and the gifts and bouquets ceased, although she caught him once or twice staring at her with wounded eyes, and she would immediately turn away or leave the room. His presence annoyed her, not because of *him*, exactly, but because it was a reminder that not only had she hurt him with her careless behaviour, but that in some way she had betrayed her love for Ashe. Although, she told herself, Ashe had never wanted her like that. He never loved her. He only had sex with her that one time to get her out of his system. And it must have worked, for he had never touched her again.

That hurt.

By the time the rosy gold of sunset turned the mountain peaks purple, she was more than ready to crawl into bed and sleep the slumber of the exhausted, until her servant woke her before dawn and it was time to start the whole process all over again.

A month went by, and then two. She was stronger, faster, more fae, she felt, although the fae around her seemed intent on reminding her of her human difference in an almost pitying way, which infuriated her.

She saw nothing of Sten and Ruby, and she was glad. The last time had been frightening, a reminder of her precarious position in the Kingdom of Stones as a guest of the One and Two. If they threw her out, where could she go? Perhaps Swirl might take her in, she thought, even if half the centaurs despised her. Perhaps she'd become a servant in another kingdom, or live in the borderlands, at the mercy of whoever might pass by. The only way to return to Earth was by the power of the Adjudicator, or perhaps Alena, and that was impossible. The Stone mage might have enough magic to send her through the veil, but the thought of living on Earth as part-fae upset her. She couldn't imagine not being able to develop the fae magic that was steadily unfolding within her. She would feel as though she were only half-alive.

Thoughts like this would race through her head, and then she would run faster, shoot further, stab her straw-filled targets with even more vigour, the adrenalin of uncertainty driving her on. At least she had her own strength, her own self to rely on.

She was in the palace grounds jogging along a snow-covered path, when she thought she glimpsed movement within a cluster of shrubs. She peered at the bushes as she ran past, not seeing anything untoward. But there were tracks ahead, footprints on the lawn, leading from one thick clump of bushes to another. She halted, breath misty in the early morning air, hand fumbling at her belt for her dagger, a new one to replace that which the centaurs had destroyed.

"Hello?" she called, but there was no response. Perhaps a guard made the footprints. A stranger couldn't infiltrate the palace, and none living within its walls would harm the guest of the One and Two. She jogged on, and soon the incident completely faded from her mind.

However, a couple of days later, she was taking the same path, and again, glimpsed movement, a shower of snow falling from a tree branch just beyond in the garden, as though someone had brushed against it.

Her immediate thought was that it was Kalin spying on her, and indignation bloomed within her. She stomped off the path to find him, intent on telling him he was being decidedly too creepy and maybe he should just leave her the fuck alone before she reported him to ... someone, anyway. She pushed through the foliage, starting with annoyance as a clump of snow went down the back of her neck. But there was no one there. She emerged on the other side of the bushes, almost tripping over a large grey rock, but stopped, taken aback.

It wasn't a rock at all, but someone wrapped from head to toe in the oddest collection of garments, someone she'd only met once before.

"Radi?"

The girl peeked up at her and weakly pulled the fabric away from her mouth and nose. She was shivering violently. "Hello."

"What are you doing here?"

"You said," Radi said, her teeth chattering so hard that Ember could barely make out the words. "That a Seed might come to the Stones."

"Well, yes, but I didn't think ... you crossed the mountains?"

Her immediate instinct was to call for a guard and a healer, but she checked herself. No fraternising between kingdoms. The One and Two had acquiesced. And besides, the Seeds had killed one of their dragons, a family member. What would it mean to Radi if she got caught? They'd probably kill her, too.

And so, she scooped Radi up in her arms and took her to the closest, safest place she could think of.

CHAPTER 19

B eyond the animal pens stood the storage sheds that held surplus animal feeds. They were a backup to the main sheds, the grains inside old and stale, only used in dire emergency if winter lingered longer than it should. Ember had never seen anyone anywhere near them.

Radi was a head and a half shorter than Ember, and she looked thinner than when Ember had last seen her, but she was still heavy, and Ember was sweating and panting by the time she reached the shed. Once inside, Ember laid the young fae on a stack of feed sacks, shrugged off her outer coat, and tucked it around her. She watched Radi anxiously, chafing her icy hands. Soon the colour returned to Radi's cheeks, and she opened her eyes.

"It's so cold," she complained, her voice barely above a whisper. "How can you bear it?"

"What are you doing here?" Ember said, ignoring the question. "How?"

"I took a boat," Radi explained with a hint of pride. "Sailed through the archipelago and around the coast."

Of course. That way she could avoid the Swords territory and cut thousands of kilometres off the trip.

"You'd have to go around the Shields' territory to land in the Stones."

"Yes." Radi's eyes shone, a smile on her lips. "And I landed on its shores and kissed the earth beneath my feet."

"But I thought it was broken and poisonous."

"When the Shields burned, everything burned. The air was noxious and nothing lived. But it's different now."

"Different? What do you mean?"

"The air is sweet again. The water runs clear. Plants have begun to grow. The Shields is returning to life."

It was as if her words were a gust of bracing air, setting the blood racing through Ember's veins, her heart thumping so loud she could feel it in her eardrums. She inhaled a slow, calming breath, willing the strange sensation away. The adrenaline and strain of trying to carry Radi after an early morning run, she supposed.

"Nature always finds a way," she said absently. "When was the last time you ate?"

"A couple of days," Radi said. "I ran out of food and couldn't forage because of all the damn snow. And I'm sick of snowdaisies. They're like chewing rope."

Ember got to her feet. "Stay here and stay hidden. I don't know what they'll do if they find you. I'll be back presently."

"No, wait," Radi protested. "Don't leave."

"Stay hidden," Ember repeated, and slipped out the door.

She tore through the gardens. The closer she got to the palace, the more courtiers, servants and guards were around, and feigning an air of casualness, she approached a lone servant and asked them for food, healing balm and a couple of warming stones.

"I'm having a little picnic," she told them, by way of excuse, but it wasn't in a servants' nature to ask questions, anyway. They returned within moments with a little basket, which Ember took with thanks before darting off again.

She looked over her shoulder several times as she hurried back to the feed shed, but it was still early and quite chilly, and the surrounding grounds were empty.

Radi had sunk into a doze and Embthanks,er shook her awake, fearful she had slipped into an unconscious state. But it was just fatigue, and as soon as Radi saw the food, she roused herself, falling on the spiced meat and buns with such enthusiasm that Ember had to slow her down, fearful she might be sick.

"Little bites, Radi," she admonished. "Chew properly."

"You sound like my mother," Radi grumbled, but she obeyed, taking her time as she swallowed some mulled wine from a flask and smiling with pleasure. "This is good."

"Anything's good when you're hungry," Ember said, recalling the pigeon she had once gulped down, charred feathers on the outside, flesh still bloody in the middle. "But yes, the Stones do a decent wine. The cider's better. It's the pure water, fresh from the mountains."

Radi chewed, swallowed, and settled back. "I think I'm full."

"Your stomach has probably shrunk. Have some more later."

Ember took the warming stones from the basket and set them on the ground. She pressed her palm against them, gave them a little nudge with her mind, and they began to glow, warming up the little room.

"Now tell me. Why did you come? Does your mother know? Did you run away?"

"My mother sent me. We pretended I had suffered a fatal accident."

"You faked your death?"

"I was torn apart by wolves," and she broke into a broad grin. "Everyone was crying and carrying on, and I was hidden under the bed with a rag in my mouth to stop myself from laughing out loud. They all said such nice things about me." She tilted her head, frowning. "Why do they say nice things about you when you're dead, and they don't when you're alive?"

Ember smiled. "I don't know. Maybe we're afraid to tell people we love them."

"Stupid." Radi took another sip of wine. The colour was back in her cheeks, and she looked much healthier. Ember made her take off her shoes to check her toes for frostbite. They weren't red or inflamed, but she rubbed in a few drops of balm just in case.

"How did you get over the border?" she said. "Our guards aren't the best, but surely the dragons would have spotted you?"

"I saw them, but they didn't see me." Radi wiggled her fingers and, in an instant, she was invisible. It wasn't a camouflage, Ember discovered when she stretched out a hand to touch Radi's torso. It was a barrier, but without the glossy appearance she was accustomed to. This barrier was completely transparent, shielding Radi from head to toe.

She reappeared, looking smug. "I've never been able to do that. But after I set foot in my homeland, it was like everything just got *better*. I think I'm taller. Do I look taller?"

Ember gave a startled laugh. For all her daring and bravery, Radi was still only a kid.

Radi sighed. "Dragons are so beautiful. And scary. I can't believe you flew on one."

"Me neither." Just the thought of Diamond brought a lump to her throat.

"Do you think, one day—?"

Ember interrupted her. "Radi, if they find you here, you're dead. The Adjudicator delivered a warning that we may not trespass into each other's territories. The Stones won't care that you're a Shield. In their eyes, you're a Seed. You're the enemy. Your presence might be enough to spark off the war. Everyone's looking for an excuse to fight."

Radi gave a sly smile, which bewildered Ember. "You don't look like a Stone."

"I'm half human. My mother or father were fae, but no one knows who they were."

Radi's eyes lit up. "I knew there was something extra weird about you."

Ember snorted. "Extra weird, huh?"

"Can you cast Stone magic?"

The question was unexpected, and she said, "Sometimes. It's hard though. I can do some things." She gestured at the warming stones with a hint of pride.

Radi snorted. "That's not Stone magic. Anyone can do that. Can you do what the Stones can do? Can you read fortunes with their runes? Can you build from rock?"

Ember flushed. "Not especially. It takes effort."

"And that's because you're human?"

Her eyes were dancing with mirth, but why, Ember wasn't quite sure.

"I suppose so."

"Are you particularly stupid?"

"I beg your pardon?"

"In your world. Are you considered to be a bit … simple?"

Ember scowled. Fae were often rude about her heritage, but she was damned if she was going to take it from a cheeky kid. "Watch it," she warned.

"I don't mean to offend you," Radi said earnestly. "It's just that it seems so obvious to me, I can't believe it hasn't occurred to you too."

"Radi, I don't know what you're talking about." Ember reached out to touch Radi's forehead, wondering if the cold and exhaustion were making her delirious.

Radi grasped her hand. For all her fatigue, her grip was strong and Ember winced as her grubby fingernails dug in. She stared at Ember intently and said slowly, "Then hear me, and understand. The Shields are returning to life."

Ember stared at her wordlessly. There was something there, something that made her stomach flutter and her heart melt. "I'm glad for you," she said faintly, and all at once a vision flashed into her head, of a majestic palace amid long avenues of trees, the red brick inlaid with tawny chips of stone, vines of flowers decorating the window frames.

Radi fumbled with the strips of fabric wrapped around her fingers to protect them from frostbite, unwinding them and letting them fall to the floor. She thrust out her hand.

Ember gazed in bewilderment at the ring on her finger, the golden gemstone glowing with a steady light. Inside the drop of amber, flecks of matter from ages past rose and fell within the stone, reminding her of the Tana the Blade and his restless shadow making the pendant she once wore flicker. She raised her eyes to Radi in confusion.

"This is my mother's ring. It was her mother's ring. The last time it glowed was when the Shields were whole."

"I don't understand."

"When the rulers and heirs were murdered, the land burned, and this stone was just a lump of brown resin. Now it glows again. It glowed when you first arrived at our camp. It glows only in your presence."

A giddy sensation took hold of Ember and, although she was already sitting, she still had to steady herself with a palm to the floor for fear of toppling over. She felt as she did when the Stone mage had once rifled through her mind and shuffled through her memories, leaving her exposed, vulnerable.

Radi's wan face split into a broad grin. "My mother knew it, and I know it too. You're an heir of the Shields. And you will bring us home."

CHAPTER 20

E mber shook her head in denial, but a kaleidoscopic of images tumbled through her mind like autumn leaves, images that were slotting into place and making the jigsaw whole. The fallen column in the dragon cave that had rebuilt itself before collapsing as if it had never been. The Shields' temple appearing out of the gloom, a shadow of itself and yet still complete. The sigil she had drawn from a memory she hadn't known she'd had. The fact that she couldn't sculpt stone, something that the smallest child could do, and yet her barriers—her *shields*—had been strong enough to withstand dragon fire. Without volition, she reached out a hand and gently touched the glowing gemstone.

A flash of fire erupted from the ring, drenching the room in a golden light that felt as warm and comforting as a drowsy summer afternoon, and at once the Radi's pale complexion brightened as colour rose to her cheeks. She drew in a sharp breath, sitting upright as though someone had just jerked a string in her back.

"You see?" she crowed. "I knew it. You're our ..." Her voice faded and an odd expression crossed her face. She hastily lowered her eyes. "Forgive me for calling you simple, My Queen."

The honorific broke through Ember's reverie, and she blinked. "I'm not your queen," she protested. "I'm just ... no one."

"But you are," Radi said calmly. "Whether or not you say so doesn't matter. You're descended from a noble line. And now you can reclaim your kingdom and we will be free."

Ember's consternation was almost palpable. "But ... it's impossible."

She longed to speak with Alena. Alena, the forest fae in the Swords' castle, would know if this was true. Surely she knew there had been a Shield living under her roof? She must have suspected something. Alena knew Ember was a fae and hadn't told her. What if she had known she was a Shield, and an heir, no less? Perhaps she hadn't known. Or perhaps she had kept quiet to save Ember's life. If Cole had found out ... Ember shivered. He would have torn her apart.

The room was too small to contain her thoughts, and she surged to her feet, longing to be outside. She needed space. She needed air.

"I must go."

Radi brightened. "At once, My Queen." She pushed back Ember's coat and struggled to get up. Ember stopped her with a sharp word.

"And where d'you think you're going?"

"I'm coming with you, of course. I'll be your ... your bodyguard. Or your assistant or something."

Despite herself, Ember was amused. "I don't need a bodyguard, or an assistant, or anything. You're not well. And I'm not traipsing off into the wilds without a plan. I don't even know if this is real."

"Yes, you do," said Radi. "You know it because it feels right, doesn't it?"

Ember chewed her lip. "In any case, you can't go wandering around. They'll kill you, do you understand? They won't care what you are and they won't listen to me. You're a stranger. You're to stay here until you've regained your strength. And then we've got to get you out of here."

"But where?" said Radi. "You can't just cast me out! I can't go back to my mother. They all think I'm dead. They'll kill both of us for lying." Her eyes were pleading, and the fingers gripping Ember's coat were white at the knuckles.

"Don't worry," Ember said, gently. "I'll figure something out. But just stay here and rest. And if anyone comes ..."

Radi smiled and vanished. "No problem."

"Don't eat everything all at once. I'll be back when I can."

"I know." Radi reappeared and settled back on the feed sacks. She looked very weary, and very young. "I'll just rest for a bit, and when you return, we can plan our escape."

Ember gave her a noncommittal smile, and opening the door a crack, checked both ways. "Lock the door behind me."

She broke into a run as soon as she hit the main path, partly to give the appearance that she was jogging, and partly because she couldn't restrain herself. She just wanted to run and run and escape the thoughts churning in her brain, but she couldn't. Still, the exercise was calming. By the time she reached the palace, she knew exactly what to do.

Going directly to her chambers, she instructed her maid to request an audience alone with the One. She wasn't particularly keen to see Ruby again. Ruby's observations regarding her ability to cast barriers accompanied with that narrowing of her eyes, meant that she had her suspicions, and Ember didn't want to have them confirmed just yet.

While the maid was gone, she threw some clothes in her pack and lashed a spear to the side. It was of a concertina type Kalin had advised was "more suitable for the ladies", a thin, lightweight pole inlaid with carved bone for decoration. At the flick of the wrist, it extended to a length more suitable for combat. Many of the ladies of the court carried them as affectation rather than for actual weaponry, and some of them were actually parasols or walking sticks. Not Ember's, though. The spear was sharpened to a point and tipped with metal blades that could lacerate flesh.

When she was packed, she employed the calming meditations she'd been taught to use before she cast a charm. There was no need to show her anxiety in front of Sten. He mustn't guess anything was amiss before she had a chance to figure all this out.

Soon the maid returned to escort her through the halls to a small sitting room, and then she waited for Sten, focusing on slow inhales and exhales, firmly banishing any thoughts of the Shields from her mind.

She bowed when Sten arrived, and she was happy to see he looked more like the kindly old uncle she was accustomed to, rather than the frightening, otherworldly creature he had become the last time she'd seen him. He sat and waved her to a seat opposite and she was careful to rest her hands in her lap with an air of calm, although she was dying to fidget. The maid returned with a small tray and poured them each a glass of wine. Ember sipped only a little, not wanting the fog of spirits to cloud her wits.

"I hear you've been diligent in your weapons' training," Sten said. "Should we station you on the battlements with the guards?"

Ember gave a startled laugh. "I just enjoy it, the exercise outdoors, you know."

"I also heard that you unceremoniously rejected Kalin's suit," Sten said with an uplifted eyebrow. "Apoli was most indignant."

"She had words with me about it," Ember admitted, a warm flush staining her cheeks. "Kalin is nice, but ... he's not quite my type. And I'm not his either, if he really thought about it."

"His blood responds to yours," Sten observed. "I'm not sure he has much say in it."

"I heard that human and fae can become ... addicted to one another. I couldn't let that happen to him." She was talking about it as though she was doing something noble, preventing Kalin from giving in to his base urges and saving him from himself, when in actual fact, she didn't want to be with him because she was in love with someone else.

All at once, the vision of Ashe sitting on a couch, her hand to his cheek, swam into her mind. It had the quality of a faint memory, of the memory of a dream perhaps, and she fancied she could hear the timbre of his voice whispering in her ear, a pleasant shiver working its way down her spine. With difficulty she dragged herself back to the present, and to Sten looking at her enquiringly.

"I beg your pardon?" she said.

"I said, why did you wish to speak to me?" His voice held a warning note of impatience.

"I wondered if you would grant me permission to visit the Stone mage. I've been having problems with some of my fae abilities, and my tutor is at a loss."

Which was true. Xarin was patient, but not particularly pleased with her progress in certain areas and now, she thought, we knew why.

Without access to Alena, the mage might be the next best thing. He had searched her mind, after all. Perhaps he already knew who she really was—assuming Radi was correct, of course. She trusted him. He wouldn't tell anyone. And perhaps he would keep Radi safe for the time being. If anyone could keep Radi from harm, it would be him. She couldn't keep Radi in her rooms. Even if she managed to smuggle Radi past the guards, her servants would find out in three seconds flat.

But no one would visit the Stone mage if they didn't have to. Although Ember found him kind with a droll sense of humour, the rest of the Stones found him aloof and daunting, his power esoteric and mighty, far surpassing their own. Even the One and Two accorded him a respect they didn't show anyone else. But for Ember, everyone's power surpassed hers, even the servants', and so she wasn't at all intimidated by the mage.

If Sten was surprised by her request, he didn't show it. He shrugged airily, as if the matter was of no consequence.

"Of course. Take some guards, servants, whoever you like to escort you. It's not an easy path, but you shouldn't have any great difficulty. And perhaps on your return, you'll be able to sculpt stone."

His eyes gleamed with amusement and Ember flushed. "You heard about my rock."

Sten chuckled. "Well, at least you tried. Perhaps those machines they have on Earth to manipulate stone have warped you in some way. The fumes, perhaps."

Ember smiled. "Perhaps." She rose and bowed to Sten. "Thank you."

He waved a hand and vanished, and she tore back to her rooms to get her pack.

CHAPTER 21

Getting Radi out of the grounds was relatively easy. Leaving without an escort had been somewhat harder. It meant she'd had to sneak out of the palace at dusk when everyone was getting ready for dinner and spend a chilly night in the shed with Radi. The young fae, excited for company, initially yapped her head off about everything and anything, before she suddenly fell asleep mid-sentence, leaving Ember to lie awake, her feet on the warming stones, wondering about the day ahead.

They left before dawn, Radi dressed in new clothes Ember had provided: warm, fleecy undergarments, and suede outer coverings with a warm hood, gloves, and knee-length boots. They tiptoed past guards who looked barely awake, Radi with her invisible barrier, Ember with her camouflage.

There wasn't much they could do about their footprints in the snow, and kept to the gravel paths, before striking out through scrub and across rocks to find the trail that led to the Stone mage's home. He lived away from society, higher in the ranges, and it wasn't long before they were puffing and blowing, dropping their disguises to make the climb easier.

"The air is thinner up here," Ember remarked to Radi. "Less oxygen. That's why it's so tiring."

Radi looked at her as if she were crazy. "It's the snow spirits stealing your breath and refusing to give it back. Look!"

She huffed out her breath, and the mist became a wraith that coiled slowly in the air. Abruptly, the mist tore and vanished, seemingly snatched in half, whisked away to who knew where.

"They're not bad spirits," said Radi. "They just like the taste of your breath."

They climbed slowly up the slope, working their way around rocky outcrops and occasionally clambering across streams that had solidified into gleaming trails of ice. The view stretched out to the horizon. To the west were nothing but frozen peaks. To the north, the faint glimmer of greenish blue ocean. The rocky ranges south gave way to the green of hills and forest. And in the east, where the sun steadily climbed, lay the smudge of brown that was the Kingdom of Shields. Only ... the brown seemed less intense, less stark. Faded, almost. A faint sparkling line lay across the landscape, as though a river was cutting its way through. *Where there is water, there is life,* she thought, and again, the blood thrummed in her veins, making her want to pick up her pace and stride up the mountain as if it were nothing.

There was Radi to think of, however. Although she had swallowed her healing draught after breakfast and had a full night's sleep, it would take time before she was fully back to health. Still, she had the advantage of growing up in the jungle. She had the wiry build of someone who spent their life outdoors, and her work as a servant—or rather, a slave—Ember corrected herself, meant she was used to manual labour and eating very little. She kept up with Ember valiantly, but Ember was careful to take breaks every hour or so, feeding her with protein-filled nut cakes and strips of cooked, dried meat, which Radi liked very much. The foods she was accustomed to were always eaten raw, and it was novel for her to eat anything cooked.

"The Seeds live very close to the world and prefer everything natural. Their magic comes from the earth that supports the roots of the great trees." And she told Ember of magical trees that grew in the southeast, trees that were so massive that a hundred fae could hold hands and still not encircle their girth.

"Then why do they want the grasslands?" Ember asked. "There are no trees—nothing like in the jungles. It's all open land."

Radi shrugged. "My mother says the Swords convinced them."

"But why? What's the point? Why would the Seeds do the Swords' bidding? Are their rulers that weak?"

Radi tried to explain. "Magic is around us all the time. When the Shields fell, much of the magic was destroyed, too. Refugees took their own, and the rest just floated on the breeze, looking for something to bond with. The mountains prevented the Stones from picking up any, but the Swords didn't have such barriers. Any leftover magic blew toward them, strengthening their position, giving the heirs an advantage. Although there's a ruler confined in the pendant, it doesn't mean much. The Blade's power was never diminished. It's just controlled by the other. Politically and magically, the Swords are still the greatest kingdom, and the Seeds know it. Better to be their friend than their enemy, yes?"

Ember's mind was racing ahead. "If the grasslands fall, the Seeds gain territory, but there's nothing in it for the Swords. Only the Adjudicator wins. He hates the centaurs."

"The Seeds need help to win," Radi said. "And they're paying the Swords to do so, with medicines, spices and enchantments."

Ember's eyes widened, remembering the ritual she had seen in the forest. She asked Radi about it, and Radi nodded, confirming her theory.

"So, the Swords' treasury swells," said Ember. "And Serafina can pay her debts."

"Yes, yes," said Radi, impatiently. "But what if the Seeds lose?"

"The Seeds border the Swords ... and their fallen magic will go ..."

"Yes." Radi said. "The Swords win. Either way, the Swords win."

They fell silent after that, packing the remains of their food carefully back into Ember's backpack, and continuing on. The day wore on, but as it approached mid-afternoon, Ember spied a thin grey spire of smoke coming from behind the rocks, and when they rounded the corner, she was gratified to see a pleasant wooden house with gables, and incongruous to the snowy surrounds, roses and honeysuckle framing the windows, bees and tiny glowing fairies darting in and out of the foliage. A little stream passed in front of the house with a wooden footbridge crossing it.

Ember went ahead, but as her foot made contact with the bridge, there came a screech that she knew well. A shadow passed over them, with the stiff breeze of enormous wings. Radi screamed, and Ember had to grab hold of her lest she sprint off back down the path again. There was an earth-shattering *whump!* behind them, and they spun to see an enormous blue dragon with teeth bared advancing upon them.

CHAPTER 22

E mber had been around dragons for months now, but she'd never met this particular beast before and it had a feral look in its eye that made her blood freeze, and her hand creep to her pack for her spear. The dragons that the palace employed in the fleet were tame—as far as dragons go—their temperaments suited for bearing the fae about. They were affectionate creatures, eager to please. This one looked wild, as though it saw anything with a heartbeat as prey. Radi looked as if she were about to bolt; the worst thing she could do. Dragons liked the hunt.

Ember's voice shook as she spoke, hoping it would understand her even if she couldn't articulate firespeech. "We visit the mage. We seek his wisdom and his favour."

The dragon drew itself up onto its hind legs and then whirled about in a tornado of blue that grew faster and faster until it resolved itself into the figure of the Stone mage himself. He smiled, and the tiny diamonds in his teeth sparkled. "If that is all you seek, then you may have it, gladly."

There came a thud as Radi collapsed to the ground in a dead faint. Ember made a helpless gesture. "She's not met many dragons. Or mages, come to think of it."

The mage smiled and crooked a finger. Radi's prostrate body rose from the ground and hovered a moment before disappearing. In response to Ember's alarmed look, he said, "She is inside." He took Ember by the elbow and led her across the bridge. "Come. I'm curious."

Ember removed her dirty boots at the door and went inside on fleece-wrapped feet. The house was warm with a crackling fire and there was the scent of something meaty and delicious drifting from a pot hanging over the coals. Radi lay on a small platform, blinking owlishly. As Ember and the mage entered the room, she struggled to sit, confused.

"Do not trouble yourself, child," the mage said. "I gave you a fright. I was enjoying a bit of exercise before dinner. No guards with you?"

"No," Ember said, taking a seat on a three-legged stool. "We had to be discreet."

The mage's gaze flicked to Radi, and his eyes widened. "Not a Stone?"

"No. A Shield, living with the Seeds."

"Brave."

"I don't think she had much choice, to be honest. But yes, brave, travelling by herself to find me."

The mage raised a curious eyebrow. "And why is that?"

"Because she thinks I'm an heir of the Shields."

It was if someone had thrown a handful of light at the mage. His face lit up, the tattooed lines across his face blazing bright red, the glittering diamonds set into his flesh becoming the colour of rubies before fading away. It had happened so suddenly that Ember was half out of her chair, scanning the room for a jug of water in case he spontaneously combusted and burned the entire cottage down, but the light faded and she sank back uneasily onto the stool.

"Of course. Of course. A Shield. That's why you were so difficult to read."

"Was I? I thought you knew everything about me when you went through my head."

The mage shrugged. "Well, one does not like to show limitations, especially in front of the One. Your fae self was easy to read, but your origins were more difficult. And you had such an affinity with the Stones! And the Swords, too, now I think on it. But your Shield self was hidden from me, from you, from everyone."

"Do you think Alena knew?"

"I don't know. Her magic is … capricious."

He spoke in the similarly dismissive way that Alena had used when she'd once referred to his magic as 'primitive', and Ember had to stifle a smile. There was history between them, she was sure of it.

He rose and went into the scullery off the main room, taking down a couple of stone bowls from a shelf. He handed one to each and bade them to help themselves to the simmering pot over the fire.

Radi gave hers a suspicious sniff before she warily spooned a mouthful. She hadn't spoken a word since they'd arrived, and Ember guessed she was still wary of the elderly fae who could turn himself into a fearsome dragon.

The soup was warm and filling, with chunks of meat that Ember didn't recognise, and she didn't ask either. She finished her bowl quickly, took the others' empty bowls to the scullery, rinsed them out with crystal clear mountain water from a dish, and then wiped them dry with a cloth. When she returned, Radi was watching her open-mouthed, as if she'd just watched Ember do three backflips in a row.

"Are you alright?" Ember asked.

"No doubt she's never seen an heir perform a menial task before," said the mage with a smile.

Radi nodded, her voice shy. "I've never seen any royalty before at all. Or snow. Or a dragon. This journey has shown me wonders."

"She can't stay at the palace. The Adjudicator has ruled …"

The mage's face closed up, his eyes becoming shuttered. "I know what the Adjudicator has *said*." He gave the word 'said,' an emphasis loaded with sarcasm. "But what one says and what one does are two entirely different things."

"I wondered if she might stay here with you. Until we can return her to the Seeds. I'm not sure how. She came by boat, but she's so much weaker now …"

Radi paled and then reddened with anger. "I cannot return! I told you that! They think I'm dead, and when they discover I'm not, they'll kill me anyway!"

"But there's nowhere else, Radi."

"We're going to the Shields! You will take your kingdom back, and we shall live for a thousand years and a thousand more in prosperity and peace! You promised!"

Ember was taken aback. "I don't think I did."

"You did, you did!" Radi was almost beside herself now, tears of childish fury rolling down her cheeks.

The mage waved a hand, and Radi's dismayed expression cleared as if it had been wiped clean. She fell back onto the cushions, her eyes fluttering closed.

"Just a gentle sleep. When she wakes, she will feel better, calmer."

Ember watched Radi anxiously and noted the deep rise and fall of her chest as she breathed slowly and calmly. Sleep was what she needed.

"While she is resting, I wonder if you would mind showing me your story once again?"

"My story?"

The mage tapped his head. "We're full of stories. I've seen many of yours already. But now that we know what's preventing me from reading you properly, perhaps you can help."

"What do you want me to do?"

"You know how your mind flexes when you create a barrier—a shield? And how you must relax it to release it?"

"Yes."

"Just relax a little more, Ember. Just a little more."

He took her hand and gazed intently into her eyes, and sparks rose and fell in his, a cascade of molten red rock that dazzled her, guiding her into a place that was soft and warm.

He shuffled through her thoughts impatiently, and she was flying backward through time, back and back, to the car crash. He had done this before, but this time, they lingered there. She felt glass, hot under her hands as she hammered her small fists against the windows, coughing. Mummy was beside her, her head lolling to one side. Blood from her hairline trickled down her cheek, and she wouldn't wake up. Daddy was asleep too, slumped over the steering wheel. Lights flashed outside, alternating red and blue. The car filled with smoke and it was hard to breathe, but a thin, glossy bubble rose around her, keeping out the fumes. Glass smashed, and she cried out as a hand snaked in, flipping open the door lock. The bubble vanished, replaced by a gust of cool air, and frantic arms dragged her out. Sparks fell around her, landing on her arms, stinging sharp as she frantically wiped at them. And then there was an explosive flash and a mighty roar, and she screamed ...

Even further back, and she was enclosed in red darkness, warm and safe. Golden trails of fire spread behind translucent eyelids, wrapping her up in a thin membrane of magic while beneath the web, her pulse thumped in tandem with another ...

The darkness faded to be replaced by a white, clear light, and Ashe was there, reaching for her hand, his expression anxious. But before his fingers could entwine with hers, her eyes flew open, and she was back in the mage's house.

The images faded. Nausea roiled in her belly, and she rubbed at her arms, still feeling the phantom bite of floating sparks.

"The child is right," the mage said. "You are an heir of the Shields."

CHAPTER 23

"How do you know?" Ember asked.

"I saw your mother. I recognised her."

Ember drew in a shaky breath, her eyes liquid with expectation. She could barely remember her mother. She just had an impression of her, a feeling of serenity, of long, dark, fragrant hair, and an easy smile.

"She was their queen's youngest grandchild. Wilo. What was it you called her?"

"Willow."

"Wild-one they used to call her, but not in front of the queen, of course." He chuckled, his eyes distant, focused on the past. "She had a reputation for mischief. Very argumentative, even from a young age. I don't know what happened to her. Everyone was told she died in an accident."

"But she had gone to Earth."

"Ran away perhaps, grew up, took a husband—many, probably—moved from place to place, not letting anyone discover she didn't age, and eventually bore a child."

"But the timing's off." Ember said, her forehead creased in thought. "The war with the Shields and the Swords happened ages ago."

"Your mother would have been at the end of her life when she had you," the mage said. "The accident wouldn't have killed her. She was a powerful Shield, able to prevent any accident with the wave of her hand. Likely she was hundreds of years old by then, and ready to die. Fae babies are born when both mother and father unite in their desire to have a child, when their wanting transcends everything else. Perhaps it was only at the end that she wanted to ensure her lineage carried on."

Unexpectedly, Ember felt tears prickle her eyes. If only she'd had the chance to know her mother and father longer.

The mage conjured a glass of sweet wine, and she sipped it gratefully.

"How long have you been visiting the Blade?"

"What?" The question had taken her off-guard. She frowned. "Oh no. It's just a dream. Ashe and I were close once. Sort of." They'd been sexually intimate, but she doubted they'd ever really been close. He'd been too accustomed to holding her away with one hand, not wanting to let her in, although she fancied she had caught glimpses of the real him, sometimes. "I think of him often. I suppose it's natural he invades my dreams, too."

The mage shook his head emphatically, his voice stern. "The pendant is a closed fortress, forged from the deepest of magic. None may enter his mansion, even if the Blade wished them to do so. The Sword may summon the Blade to wield his power, but even the Sword must first knock and wait. You haven't been dreaming, Ember. What you experienced was a type of astral travel, when the essence of oneself is free to glide upon the wind between worlds."

Ember's heart raced. She had actually been there? "The first time I saw him was when I fell from Diamond's back. I hit my head. I was out of it for a while ..." She thought back but couldn't really remember the words she and Ashe had exchanged. It was like trying to recall a dream, fragments of conversation, an impression of him rather than an actual memory. "The second time was when a shadow snake thing attacked me."

"So, when you are under extreme circumstances, you turn to the Blade for help."

"Are you sure? I can't remember it properly."

"You can break his shield," the mage confirmed with a nod. "And he lets you."

"But only by accident. Do you think I could do it on purpose?"

"You can try."

She closed her eyes, willing herself to be at Ashe's side. She squeezed her eyes tighter, fists clenching, a frown creasing her forehead as she strained to make her mind flex.

"Don't shit on my rug," the mage said, amused.

Her eyes popped open, and she let out her breath in a startled laugh. "I can't believe you just said that." Her concentration broken, she felt too weary to try again. The fire crackled as a log shifted. Radi sighed in her sleep and turned onto her side. "If the Swords find out about a Shields' heir running around, what will they do?"

"They will kill you."

"Right. Well, it's not as if that's new."

In the mage's presence, she felt no fear. And besides, there were the mountains to protect her, the dragons, and the might of the Stones.

Although, if a young fae could find her way in, and to the *palace* no less, how much easier would it be for a powerful fae like Serafina?

"Does the Blade know about your mother?"

"I don't think so. Only you. And her."

As one, they turned to look at Radi's sleeping form. Her face in restful repose, she looked as innocent as a baby.

The mage clicked his tongue. "You're right. She must stay here."

He suddenly cocked his head as though listening for something and flashed in a swirl of grey to the bookcase standing in the corner of the room. He took down a small stone bowl and flashed back to the table, setting it between them.

"Is something wrong?"

For the first time since she had met him, his habitually calm demeanour was agitated, his expression clouded. He didn't answer her, instead tipping the bowl and dropping a handful of grey stones carved with white symbols into his hand. He rubbed them between his palms, his lips moving soundlessly, and threw them back into the bowl. He swirled them around the bowl once, twice, and then dumped the stones onto the table, studying them intently. Ember had seen the Stones do this before, although their seeing stones were usually made of obsidian etched in gold, much more showy than these modest pieces. Many carried them out of affectation because only a few could use them to interpret the future, Sten among them.

Ember studied the stones closely, but they held no great meaning for her. The mage swept them into the palm of his hand and returned them to the bowl. His voice was quiet as he said, "The Swords march to the Seeds in stealth, as the Seeds prepare their fighters. The battle for the Free Grasslands begins."

CHAPTER 24

E mber scrambled down the path toward the palace as quickly as she could without turning an ankle on the rocky slope. Both she and the mage had agreed to let Radi sleep, forestalling any protest to remain with Ember. The mage would convince her to stay with him for the time being until Ember could ... could what?

She was at a loss.

The idea of marching to the Shields' broken territory and proclaiming her right to it was laughable. She had no army, no allies, no protection. The Swords would fall on her faster than a duck on a slug, and she couldn't see the Stones risking themselves to fight for her. Besides, the land was empty, and she was only half-fae. She was a half-queen of nothing.

And so, as she had when alone in the wilderness, she cast the long-range problem out of her mind to focus on the issue directly in front of her. The Swords were sneaking into the Seeds' territory in direct defiance of the Adjudicator's ruling to attack the centaurs. She couldn't do anything to stop it, but perhaps the Stones might.

The trip was much faster on the way back, all downhill with terror nipping at her boots. When she arrived at the palace, the guards bade her go to the throne room. There courtiers and advisors stood in huddles, conversing in low, anxious voices. The mage had already sent word that a contingent of the Swords army—five hundred of them—were advancing quickly through their southern forest, aiming for a bridge that spanned the border. The size of the force showed this wasn't a covert operation, but neither were they prepared to commit their entire army.

Ruby and Sten were embroiled in a hissed conversation and Ember feared to approach in case they accused her of eavesdropping again, but then Ruby's voice grew strident in exasperation and the room fell silent.

"We cannot interfere! You cannot think this is a good idea."

Sten's jaw was set in obstinate annoyance. "The Seeds murdered our baby, our darling Diamond. Have you forgotten so soon?"

"Of course not—" Ruby began.

"The Adjudicator does nothing to stop the Swords from marching to the Seeds for war, and yet his hand is at my throat for visiting an ally?" Sten's voice became a roar, and the floor trembled.

"We have our people to consider," Ruby insisted. "We cannot thrust ourselves into someone else's grievance."

"And we should hide behind our mountain ranges as the Skies hide within their towers? We should do the Adjudicator's bidding whilst he tears the country out from under us?"

The chandeliers swayed and tinkled as an icy breeze swirled through the room. Ruby pursed her lips. Ember suddenly realised she was standing in front of the dais alone, the other fae having slowly withdrawn to the edges of the room with heads bowed to avoid making eye contact with the One who seemed on the verge of exploding.

"Get out," Ruby snapped. Everyone scuttled from the room. Ember hastened to join them, but "Not you."

Ruby crooked a finger. Ember slid toward her throne as if the floor were made of ice, and she windmilled her arms to keep her balance. Her first instinct was to lash out with a shield, and she felt her mind flex as if longing to do so, but she restrained herself, controlled it. The last thing she wanted was to raise Ruby's ire in tandem with Sten's.

The ice beneath her feet became tiles again, and she braced herself, hands clasped behind her back, eyes on her boots, wishing she'd had a chance to wash and rest first. Her boots and the lower legs of her pants were dirty, and she had a gnawing suspicion she smelled of nervous sweat. "Your Majesties."

"No doubt you would like us to intervene?" Her voice was as smooth as silk. Ember could feel it wrapping around her like a ribbon, coaxing her. Ruby was using a charm on her, some kind of truth telling spell, but she could resist it. It would just take a little *flex*.

"I don't want the centaurs to die. They are a free people and deserve to live their lives in peace their homeland, as any of us would. What the One and Two choose to do is their decision alone."

Ruby's eyes narrowed. "You do not wish for the Stones to come to harm at the Swords' hands? At the hands of the Adjudicator?"

Ember's head came up at that. "No! Of course not! You have been my refuge, my most gracious hosts. I would never wish harm on this kingdom, or any other. But the Swords overreach, and they're being driven by the Adjudicator, and if they are not stopped ..." She paused with a rueful shrug. "I cannot think this is good for Esha."

"You have no feeling for the Swords? You're not bound to them by loyalty ... or love?"

"I—" She hesitated, wanting nothing more than to confess the truth, that she was indeed in love, in love with the Blade. But she could resist it. She had to. She forced herself to answer, flexing the shield in her mind, trying not to react to the sudden slashing pain in her mouth as the lie fell from her lips. "No."

Ruby nodded slowly, and the ribbons of her truth spell slid away. Ember tried not to show her relief. She didn't know how long she could resist a real interrogation. Even that one lie had felt like broken glass slicing at her tongue.

But Ruby seemed satisfied with her answer, and turned to Sten. "Then what say you, my love?"

Sten's eyes glittered. "I say we fuck them up."

CHAPTER 25

The plan wasn't just to prevent the Swords from joining the Seeds. It was to send a clear message to the whole of Esha that war was not tolerable, and that the Stones were taking charge, doing everything in their power to maintain peace. Braving the wrath of the Swords was reckless, but the status they would gain if successful was worth it, or so Sten insisted.

Ember assumed they would take the fleet. A single dragon was enough to make an enemy quake in its boots, much less a horde of them. But Sten, although he didn't say it, was loath to lose another. A single poisoned arrow had brought Diamond down. He had no intention of losing others. Besides, waiting for them to arrive, outfitting them and flying them to the bridge would take far too long. Ember suspected pride too, kept him from using the fleet. He wanted to prove the Stones could stand alone, army against army. Instead, he employed the mage to find a faster way. The Swords were already a day's march ahead. The Stones couldn't waste any time.

The guards weren't old enough to have fought in the terrible war between the Shields and the Swords. All were unseasoned warriors, accustomed to guarding walls that were never breached, tranquil in the knowledge that ice and fire were at their backs keeping intruders out. They were excited and fearless: young, beautiful fae with spotless armour glittering in the morning light, boasting how they would win honour for their families and their kingdom.

Ember, watching them, couldn't help a feeling of trepidation. Unlike the Stones, the Swords trained constantly; the battle for the crown was part of their very identity. To be chosen for one of the heirs' teams was the highest honour, and they started training as children for the chance to be selected. The guards were disciplined soldiers, the male courtiers and many of the females practised in the fighting arts. Even the villagers carried weapons as a matter of rote. And the Stones? The Stones liked to drink and dance and skate.

Ember, clad in a light, yet sturdy, chain mail garment under her tunic, gathered with the others on the concourse in the lower garden. She carried her spear, her dagger was slung into her belt, and the armourer had given her a quiver and bow. It was too big for her, but there weren't any left in her size.

Under the mage's instruction, servants constructed an intriguing stack of applewood branches balanced on great chunks of crystal: amethyst, carnelian, quartz. She hadn't had a chance to speak with him privately, but when she caught his eye, he nodded, by which she assumed Radi was still safe in his home.

Sten's voice carried over the crowd. He was excited, jovial, eager to be underway, while beside him, Ruby was more taciturn, still and silent. Ember wondered at the wisdom of both going together. Perhaps one should stay home in case the other fell? And then she recalled Ashe's words: "One day both will die and then a new One and Two will be chosen." Perhaps this would be the day.

Kalin stood with a knot of soldiers, proud and elegant, checking his sword blade for flaws, although she knew he always kept his weapons in perfect condition. He'd made no move toward Ember since the day she'd told him she wasn't interested. Although she was relieved that he'd been a gentleman about it, she missed his easy friendship. She'd ruined that with her craven wanting; had played with his heart with as little regard as a child carelessly breaking a toy, and she regretted it, as much as she was glad to be free of him.

She caught sight of Apoli sashaying through the crowd toward Kalin, and he greeted her with a warm smile. She tucked a snowdaisy into his tunic pocket, and his lips found hers. They clung together, and when they parted, there were tears in Apoli's eyes, and her lower lip trembled. Kalin entwined his fingers through hers, drew her close and whispered in her ear, and despite her obvious grief and fear at his leaving, she laughed. They made a fine couple, Ember thought, and it was with a mingled feeling of relief and perverse disquiet that she realised Kalin had moved on.

Intent on Kalin and Apoli, she started as her tutor, Xarin, came to her side. He nodded at the pyre. "It's called shadowing. The mage will use the power of the mountains to cast a shadow and send us to the border. It hasn't been done in an age. Likely he had to research in the library for instruction, for I doubt he would have—"

"Is it like going through a column?" Ember cut in, apprehensive. She hated travelling through the columns. It was like being thrust into a black tornado.

"Easier than that. Your stone blood responds to the stone shadow and you become a part of it." Xarin looked at her appraisingly. "Your human blood may prove a hindrance."

Yeah, thought Ember, her heart sinking. *And the fact I'm not actually a Stone.*

"Are you sure you want to come? There is no shame in staying."

Ember shook her head and cast a quick, sideways glance at the Two, every inch the militant queen in gleaming silver armour. "No. I'm coming." She wanted to prove herself to Ruby, if only so she had a place to rest her head at nights.

The mage flicked his palm outward toward the mound of firewood and it burst into flame. All chatter ceased and, in the silence, a chilly breeze slid through the terraces with an ominous low moan. The mage chanted a few words, and the flames became a brilliant blue. He took a vial from somewhere about his person, and unstoppered it. He tossed the contents at the fire, and drops of shining red hovered over the flames before slowly descending. As the liquid hit the flames, the fire gave a terrifying screech and flames whirled and congealed into the visage of a dragon, jaw wide, a red fire boiling in the back of its throat. Ember's vision swam. The mage had become a column of flame shooting up toward the sky. But no, he was still a stooped figure in grey robes, and the fire was just a fire, a bonfire to toast marshmallows, the sweet smell of burning applewood scenting the air.

All at once the flames went out, and the coloured crystals turned grey. The shadow that streamed before the pyre was a pool of inky black, a black that seemed to suck the sunlight away into itself, a black hole absorbing all.

The mage beckoned to the nearest guard, and without hesitation, the guard walked across the shadow and vanished. A line quickly formed behind him, and one by one, they went through. Sten and Ruby walked hand in hand, waving carelessly at those watching, and

Ember wished she had someone to hold onto, too. She walked toward the shadow, suddenly afraid. It was so dark, blacker than black, and all at once, a childish fear of the dark stirred somewhere in her memory.

As she passed the mage, she said, "Are you coming through?" and he shook his head.

"I must stay and maintain it from this end, else you'll not be coming back again." He placed a hand on her arm. "Put up your barriers. This will not be pleasant."

"Will I—" she couldn't finish the question. *Will I live?*

The mage shrugged as if she had spoken aloud. "Put up your barriers," he repeated. "Hold onto them tight."

She nodded, a lump coming into her throat. The line was moving steadily. She was getting closer to the shadow with every step. Finally she was at the front and, drawing a deep breath, she stepped through.

Chapter 26

E mber had been blasted by dragonfire, but it was nothing like this. She had travelled through the columns in a whirling maelstrom of darkness, but this was not that either.

This was like being crushed by a steamroller. All at once, she understood what it was to be part of a shadow. It was to be two-dimensional, flat, to have her light extinguished. Panic and fear were all-consuming as a heavy weight compressed her, smothering her. She couldn't breathe, for her lungs wouldn't expand. Her heart couldn't beat, her brain couldn't think. She couldn't struggle against it because she had no strength. All she had were her shields, and she held onto the gloss of them as tight as she could, drawing them around her like a cocoon. She had once learned that a caterpillar didn't just grow wings and turn into a butterfly. It disintegrated into a puddle of goo before rebuilding itself from nothing, reforming, growing, expanding. This felt like that. She was nothing, and then she became something.

Finally, she had form, and then she had feeling, as a bitter freezing wind cut through her. Eventually she became aware that she was being held, and she could hear voices, could see the black behind her eyelids. Something was pressed to her lips, and then flowed in a thin stream down her throat; a healing draught of some kind. As it worked its way into her, the sensation of cool water replaced the memory of crushing suffocation, and she coughed, opening her eyes.

Kalin was supporting her, his eyes worried. "Ember. Come on now."

She couldn't help it. She burst into helpless tears and was then surprised that she still had liquid within her, that it hadn't been pulverised to nothing. The conversation continued overhead as she shuddered, drawing in deep breaths to fill her lungs as much as she could.

"What's wrong with her?" Kalin said.

"I'm not sure." It was Xarin's voice, vaguely disapproving. "I told her that her mixed blood might prevent the shadowing, but she was determined to come."

"She is brave," Kalin said.

"Or stupid. We need everyone in the fight, not looking after a helpless human."

Ember looked up indignantly at that. Xarin was smiling slyly at her. How provoking of him. All she wanted was to cry with strong, comforting arms around her, and now she had to be brave and prove him wrong.

She blinked back her tears and scrubbed at her face. "I apologise. It was ... a strong sensation."

Kalin helped her to her feet, and she leaned on him for a moment or two while she found her balance. She gave him a wan smile. "Thank you."

"Of course." He bowed his elegant courtier's bow, his eyes passing over her as lightly as if she were a stranger. "I wish you good fortune in the battle ahead."

He disappeared into the crowd and she sank to a crouch, pretending she was doing up the laces of her boot, but in truth, to disguise her wobbly legs.

The telltale sepia tone of the countryside told her they had successfully travelled to the border between the Seeds and Stones. The shadow fell behind her, cast by a rocky hillock, and one by one, the Stones walked out of it, as casual in their arrival as they had been in their leaving.

A chasm yawned ahead, a rickety wooden swing bridge linking the two cliffs. When she had the strength to stand, she moved as close as she dared to the edge to look down. It was a long way to fall. Sharp, broken rock littered the banks of a sullen, slow-moving river at the bottom. In the odd environment of the border, with the strange muting of sound and the sensation of moving in slow motion, she felt it were just a dream, and if she cast herself into the depths of the canyon she'd merely float, or turn into a teapot or something. On the opposite side, the sepia border coloured a wide strip of ground before becoming the dark green of the Swords' forest. Their army was in those emerald depths, approaching closer and closer ...

"Are you quite well?" Ruby's voice interrupted her reverie.

Ember started and hastily made a bow. "I am well, Your Majesty. Not too fond of heights."

"Or shadowing?"

"I found it difficult. My tutor said it was the human bit. As always."

Ruby made no comment on that. She gestured toward the forest opposite. "The Swords are in there somewhere. We will stop them before the bridge, and if they make it over, the reserve will take them."

"And the Seeds?"

They turned to study the land behind them beyond the sepia border; an undulating row of green hills with thick forest on either side.

"The Seeds don't have soldiers," Ruby said dismissively. "They're just a ragtag bunch of forest dwellers who'll win battles by sheer numbers, swarming like rats over a carcass, not by strategy or discipline. Besides, they've no need to send an army to welcome the Swords. Perhaps a diplomatic welcoming committee. They'll not be able to sneak up on us without the rear guard seeing. And then we fight."

Ember wondered at the wisdom of placing themselves between two rival kingdoms, but Sten and the commander of the guards insisted the advantage was theirs. The Swords would quail in the face of a surprise ambush and attack. Besides, a single Stone was worth five of the Swords and at least fifty of the Seeds. Everyone knew that.

"And what of the Adjudicator? Will he not be urging them on?"

"He cannot be seen to be taking sides—even if we all know which side he is really on. You will stay here with the reserve. The archers will have need of you."

Privately, Ember doubted that, given that the weight of the bow already dragged at her back as if she were toting a bag of rocks, but she said, "Yes, Your Majesty. I'll do everything I can for the honour of the Stones."

Ruby swung away toward Sten, the crowd parting and bowing as she passed. A blaze of beige sparks overhead caught Ember's attention. Several firebirds were slowly winging their way across the gorge, the atmosphere dragging at their wings. But their brown feathers turned back to their habitual red colour as they left the border, and they sped up again in a shower of fiery sparks. A fae opened a wicker basket and more birds took flight, this time toward the Seeds.

The commander split the force, sending the majority across the bridge, Kalin at the head. It took a long time to cross, for there was only room for two abreast. The bridge creaked alarmingly as it rocked and swayed under their boots, making Ember wonder how long it had been hanging there—and how much longer it had left.

The force spread along the bare edge of the cliff. It would be better if they could slip into the forest itself, but that was Swords' territory and Sten wanted the freedom and anonymity of fighting in no-man's-land.

The archers on Ember's side arrayed themselves along the chasm, bows at the ready. Ember surveyed the distance, wrinkling her nose. She'd have a job getting her arrows over the width of the chasm, let alone hit anyone with them. She'd be lucky if she didn't hit her own soldiers in the back.

Xarin stood with the other tutors, powerful all of them, but none in the same league as the Stone mage. They huddled in a group, gesticulating and planning. The occasional laugh drifted to her, and she wondered what it was they found so funny. Ruby and Sten stood at the rear, bickering. Nearby, a guard stood by the shadow, looking none too happy, for his only job was to ensure someone didn't fall into it by accident.

It wasn't long before the first of the birds returned, gliding down to land on its handler's outstretched arm. The bird broke into a melodious warble (a warble that sounded nothing like the angry squawking of the firebird pet that had ditched Ember for Swirl) and the handler hurried over to the commander. The message was quickly relayed around the troops; the Swords' guards were moving at speed, and were less than an hour away.

One by one, the birds who had flown to find the Swords reappeared, to be fed and caged, but the birds who had departed for the Seeds didn't return. The handler faced their territory and pursed his lips as though whistling. The sound wasn't audible to Ember, but all the caged birds flapped and twittered with excitement.

And then everything went quiet. Sounds were muted anyway, but now there was nothing, no stray bits of clanging metal, no voices, no squawking, no chatter. Everyone just waited, and Ember wondered if they could hear the pulse of their heartbeats thumping in their ears as she could. She gripped her bow, an arrow at the ready.

There was a harsh crackle of branches and the low rumble of many feet pushing through the forest. As the first Sword emerged from the treeline, a Stone struck him down. Three more met the same fate, and the rest of the Swords must have realised what had happened, for they immediately fanned out, emerging from the trees at different points.

Several of the Stones broke away from the primary force to engage them and the archers drew, fired high over the fighting lines toward the treeline. Ember copied them, her fingers cold on the bow. Her first arrow didn't even clear the gorge, and she clucked her tongue in red-cheeked embarrassment. When she tried again, her arrow only just missed one of their own soldiers.

The Swords suddenly surged from the treeline, and the fighting began in earnest. From behind her came a shout of alarm, and she spun to see a flock of metal birds—no, *blades*—spinning through the air, whirling end over end, obviously enchanted, for they showed no sign of slowing and were unerringly focused on Sten and Ruby.

CHAPTER 27

There was a tingling flash between her shoulder blades as, without thinking, she flung up a shield around the One and Two. The tutors cast more barriers until the shield looked like several panes of thick glass. The blades hit the barrier and shattered, the metal shards turning to silver-grey dust. Xarin gave Ember a quick nod of congratulation; he had recognised hers as the first.

The rear guard drew their bows and shot, taking down the first wave of Seeds as they tore down the hill before they could even hit the sepia grounds of the border, while the tutors cast a shield along the borderline. The Seeds halted, their faces warped in the shimmering light of the barrier. Outnumbered by the Stones, with apparently no other weapons besides the flying blades, they quickly regrouped, retreating to cluster together at the base of the hill. They were unprepared to see an army waiting for them, but they gave no reaction of urgency or dismay. After the initial bout of blade throwing, they simply waited out of bowshot, leaving their fallen comrades in crumpled heaps.

Ember, feeling her shield skills would probably be of more use to the tutors than the archers, left her post and headed for Xarin to see what she could do to help, but Ruby beckoned to her as she passed.

"Was that your barrier?"

"Yes," Ember said, with a hopeless grimace. "I fear I'm more of a hindrance to the archers."

"And yet, you tried anyway." Ruby's tone was warm, and Ember looked at her, surprised. It had been a long time since she had seen Ruby show her anything toward her but a vague suspicion.

After a quick word with Xarin, Ember threw her power into maintaining the shield around Sten and Ruby, leaving the tutors to turn their attentions elsewhere. Sten observed the waves of Swords breaking through the forest with barely disguised concern. "They keep coming."

He didn't say what was patently obvious; the Swords were far more competent than the Stones. They had quickly recovered from the ambush and easily swung into attack formations honed by years of constant drilling. Their magical fae cast shimmering spells that made the Stones' die with their hands at their throats as if trying to peel away the invisible hands that were holding them, and the tutors were hard pressed to fight them off and keep their shields maintained at the same time. They were humbled into defence, while the Swords were relentless in their attack. Little by little, inch by inch, they forced the Stones back toward the cliff edge.

The commander sounded the horn, and those who could, ran for the bridge.

"We'll bring it down," Sten said, his frustration evident. This wasn't how it was supposed to go. They were supposed to have stopped the Swords in their tracks, and now they were forced to run for their lives.

"Not yet," Ruby said, watching the retreat with anxious eyes. The bridge was swinging wildly, the weight of trampling feet making the beams and supports creak dangerously.

"We cannot wait."

The Swords had formed a thick line and were pushing forward. A Stone guard was fighting desperately at the edge of the cliff. His foot slipped back, finding nothing but thin air. He fell with a scream, tumbling down, down into the rocky depths of the gorge. His fall seemed to release Ruby from her inertia and she reached for Sten's hand, clasping it tight.

A glowing light came from their palms, swiftly enveloping their arms and up over their torsos until both were drenched in shimmering light. Wings erupted from their backs, Sten in a silver grey, Ruby's in dark crimson.

The pebbles on the earth's surface trembled and Ember felt a rumble up through her boots. Cracks split the cliff face on the opposite side of the gorge, and a section of it slumped, sending fae screaming to the bottom, Swords and Stones alike. Ember watched, dismayed. The One and Two had no qualms about murdering their own. Make it over the bridge, or die.

In the middle of the bridge, a desperate sword fight was underway between two guards on either side. The Sword took the Stone's knees out from under him with one vicious slash, and kicked his teetering body over the side, before moving forward to engage the next. The bridge swung with their exertion, the rope supports screaming in protestation. One of the wooden slats of the deck came loose and fell away, dropping soundlessly into the gorge.

There was a shift in the atmosphere, one which everyone felt, for there was a pause, a hitch in the commotion, and an icy shiver went down Ember's back as Cole emerged from the treeline and into the fray.

Ember blinked. No, she was mistaken. It was Serafina, clad in silver armour, her long golden hair tied in a braid which swung jauntily, as if she were out for an afternoon stroll. The Swords parted for her as she passed among their ranks, and even at that distance, the malevolent glare she cast toward Sten and Ruby was unmistakable.

It wasn't clear if the One and Two even noticed her. They were fully entranced by their magic and in the havoc they were causing. Rocks tore themselves from the cliff, tumbling into the gorge, and then came a terrific jolt which knocked soldiers off their feet. As they stumbled to regain their balance, Serafina drew herself up and raised her arms.

Lightning flashed, followed by a ghostly after-print of green, which made it difficult to see clearly. When Ember's vision returned, he was the first she saw.

Ashe.

His jaw was set, his sword whirling as he cut down one Stone after another, with as little regard as if they were dried leaves scattering in the wind. He towered over everyone, grown by at least two metres since she last saw him. Serafina was wielding the Blade, and he was an ogre of destruction and death. A trail of bloodied corpses lay behind him, and his eyes were blank as he advanced toward the bridge. The Swords fell back, letting him through, and then regrouped behind him. The air was thick with arrows, but with the shimmering shields rising and falling as power was first held and then subdued, few were finding their mark, and none made it anywhere near Ashe.

Light still enveloped Sten and Ruby, the strength of their power rising them up as they forced their magic through the earth. Another earthquake, and more rocks fell into the gorge.

Ignoring the bridge completely, Ashe stepped off the side of the cliff, his raven wings snapping wide. He flew alongside the bridge, his sword whirling. The Stones tried to dodge, but there was nowhere to go, and their lifeblood poured through the slats. He landed lightly on the Stones' side, encased in a shimmering barrier as his sword flashed. Stones fell, powerless against his onslaught.

"Ashe!" Ember cried. "Stop!"

He couldn't possibly have heard her, for a cacophony of screams and agonised cries filled the muted space, and yet his head flicked up and he saw her. His eyes, once blank with the force of Serafina's will, came into focus. He hesitated, his sword falling slack in his hand, and then —

A flash of white light and she was at his side in his mansion. He lay on the couch, his face pale and drained. Shadows wreathed his eyes and his once healthy complexion held a sickly pallor.

"Ember. Why are you with the Stones?" His voice was a croak, hardly more than a whisper, his face concerned.

"I was safe there." She sank to her knees next to him, smoothed his hair back from his forehead. Although he looked pale and cold, his skin was feverish under her hand. "You must stop. You're killing us."

"I can't stop it. I can't stop her. I am hers to wield."

"You must, Ashe. The Swords cannot help the Seeds make war on the grasslands. You never wanted that."

He frowned, as if trying to remember. "Yes."

"Then try, Ashe. Try."

His expression cleared, as if he was seeing her for the first time. The ghost of a smile tugged at his lips. "You look well. Life in the mountains agrees with you."

She shrugged lightly. "They have been very kind." She was about to expand, but stopped, recalled to the predicament of her situation. He didn't know she was fae, and if he suspected she was a Shield, if *Serafina* suspected ...

His gaze skated over her again, piercing, and a warmth bloomed in her cheeks at his appraisal, but then he grimaced and sucked in a sharp breath as if struck by a sudden pain.

"What it is?" She didn't know what to do for him, and her hands fluttered over him, stroking his forehead, patting his chest, clutching his hands. She felt helpless.

"She makes me kill them. Every life taken tears at me." His knees jerked upward and his body curled into a ball. "She forces me." The words were a tortured groan, and knotted veins stood out in his neck and fists.

"Your own people are dying too. Sten and Ruby are united, and they have the strength of mountains inside them. They will not surrender. You *must* resist her, Ashe."

Her voice rang through the room, strong and persuasive, chipping at the power of the Sword that held him entranced. She leaned over him and kissed him, and despite his weakness, he kissed her back, hard and hungry, hands sliding into her hair to bring her closer, closer. Heated desire rose in her and a shield bloomed fluid and silky, passing from her mouth to his. She felt it slither into him, felt him shudder. She pulled back, her eyes liquid with wanting, eloquent with passion.

"Resist her. For me."

He nodded, and a new look of determination came into his eyes, a rush of colour flaring in his pallid cheeks. "Yes. Wake up."

The muted clamour of the border came back to her in a rush. The cliff on the other side was slowly collapsing, sending Swords and Stones alike sliding toward the edge, while Serafina hovered in the treeline of her own territory, safe from the chaos.

Ashe stood just a few metres from Ember, the two separated by a thick mass of soldiers. A circle of bodies lay heaped around him, his sword still spun in his hands, and yet, even as the Stones guards advanced on him, he didn't strike. He parried and swung, defending himself but not attacking, and the effort it cost him not to kill was etched plainly on his strained face, and in his shield, which was now ragged and torn.

The ground beneath Ember's feet jerked as if alive. The anchors holding the swing bridge in place gradually forced themselves upward out of the earth, wrenching themselves free, and then the bridge fell in a slow, graceful arc, soldiers spilling off it with screams as it smashed against the cliff face.

The Swords' archers unleashed a volley of bolts. She heard them before she saw them, an eerie, screaming whistle that froze her in her tracks. She was suddenly reminded of the shaft that had killed Diamond, and of the one that had taken her in the shoulder, of hot, unrelenting agony as it split muscle and tendon. But Ashe was there, rising in front of her, his wings outstretched, shielding her from the onslaught. His gaze caught Ember's and held for an endless moment.

And then a Stone spear hurtled through the air, piercing his broken shield, and with an agonised cry he was thrown backward, back into the gorge.

CHAPTER 28

A wave of horror came over Ember and she stumbled forward to the edge, finally remembering to throw up a barrier to protect her from stray missiles. His dark shadow skimmed the bottom of the gorge, flew along the ravine and up the other side. Her relief was overwhelming, and as she turned away, she had to fight to school her expression, to appear as disappointed as all the others.

With the defeat of the Blade and the loss of the bridge, the Swords' guards seemed to lose heart, retreating into the trees. The Seeds too, were strolling back up the hill, apparently unconcerned that their meeting with the Swords had gone awry. They just looked happy to be leaving.

Sten and Ruby launched one final attack at the cliff face, tearing away more chunks until they had eroded the gorge right back to the Swords' forest. They sank to the ground, hands still clasped, the light of their magic suffusing their faces for one last glorious moment before it vanished.

Ruby sagged against Sten's shoulder, and he held her close, calling for a guard. One was at his side in moments, sweeping Ruby into his muscular arms.

She struggled against him, and Ember caught the word "No, put me down, I won't go!" but at a nod from Sten, the guard strode to the shadow and they disappeared inside.

Serafina emerged from the trees. A shadow bloomed around her and vanished—Ashe had returned to her side. Ember wondered with a thrill of fear how much Serafina knew about the part he had played in their defeat. Serafina's rage was a tangible thing, snapping and crackling about her in violent sparks of temper. She threw her head back and shrieked, and a circle was laid flat around her, trees, bushes, her own guards, everything a smoking charred mass.

She glared across the gorge and her eyes met Ember's. Before Ember could duck or turn away, recognition illuminated her face, her mouth dropping with displeasure. She flickered, and there stood Cole, his eyes wide, his face pale. It was just a fleeting moment, and then Serafina reappeared.

She shrieked at them, her voice carrying easily over the distance. "Your interference shall cost you dearly. The Stones shall crumble and fall beneath our displeasure."

"Bring it," muttered Sten under his breath, and he sank to one knee. With the last of his strength, he slammed his fist on the ground. The earth shuddered beneath Serafina's feet and she swayed, almost toppling over the edge, before she sharply clapped her hands and vanished.

Sten gave a roar of triumph. "We have the day!"

There was a ragged cheer, and weary guards began moving toward the shadow that would take them home. Ember took one look at its inky blackness and blanched. She was so tired, so overwrought. The thought of undergoing that crushing terror again was enough to bring on a panic attack.

Sten beckoned to Xarin, and the tutor came slowly forward. He was weary too, weary with the strain of holding a shield the Seeds didn't bother to breach, and of casting spells the Swords' mages could dismantle in moments. Like the Swords' soldiers, their mages were just *better*. How fortunate the Blade had lost heart, taking the will of his people with him.

"Take Ember," Sten said. "No point her dying on the trip home."

Xarin pasted on a reassuring smile, which did little to reassure her. He scooped up a handful of earth and gravel and pressed it into her palm. "Take the power of stone with you."

She threw up a shield, as thick as she could make it, and Xarin forced his magic between the molecules of hers, strengthening it until it was unyielding. They stepped into the blackness together and she clung to her shields and to the earth in her palms. Their barrier shuddered and cracked under the onslaught of the suffocating weight, and she tried to scream but she couldn't draw breath. It shattered to pieces just as they emerged on the other side, and Xarin had to grab her before she fell.

"I didn't realise it was so bad for you," he said.

She wiped her mouth, suddenly aware she was drooling. "Never again."

Anxious courtiers thronged the concourse, and the wounded lay everywhere, healers attending them. Xarin helped her to a terrace before he left to help the others, and she sat, closed her eyes, and breathed. Within moments, Apoli was at her side, her beautiful face lined with strain.

"Did you see Kalin? Was he alright?"

"I—I don't know." Ember tried to think back. The last time she'd seen Kalin, he'd been leading the guards over the bridge. She'd lost sight of him after that.

Apoli scanned the crowd desperately, and Ember caught her hand. "He might still be there. Many were still there."

Apoli shuddered. "I fear many will remain there, too."

She vanished into the crowd. The commotion was becoming too much. With everyone occupied helping the wounded and relaying news, the best thing she could do was get out of everyone's way. Dragging herself to her feet, she moved out of the garden, and joined the others heading up to the palace. When she got to her chambers, she was gratified to find a hot bath already drawn, and soaked for a long while, trying to put the events of the day out of her mind. She didn't want to think about the slaughter and the fae crumpled and broken at the bottom of the ravine, nor about Ashe, his face alien and blank as he cut down the Stones with no mercy and no regret.

Steam rose from her flesh as she finally hopped out of the tub, and the maid appeared with a container of healing balm. She insisted on rubbing it into every inch of Ember's skin, and Ember felt her muscles relaxing under her ministrations. The maid brought a tray, and once she had eaten, Ember dismissed her and hopped into bed, wanting the day to finally be over.

But sleep was elusive. There was nothing to prevent memories crowding her mind, and nothing to do but examine them and try to make sense of them.

Cole had gone nowhere. He was inhabiting the same space as Serafina. He'd probably done so since the day she won the crown. Ember had glimpsed him before and thought it was only a glamour, Serafina taking on the guise of Cole before revealing her true self. But now she saw they were two sides of the same coin, each a parasite of the other. Serafina was stronger than Cole, though. Certainly, it was she who showed her face more often.

And what did it mean for Ashe if there were *two* draining his energy, two separate fae purporting to be the Sword? Was that why he was so ill? So weak? She recalled the words he'd spoken the first time she'd visited him in his white mansion: *"She is the sun and the moon in one."* So perhaps Ashe suspected, but he didn't know for sure.

"It can't be allowed," she said aloud. "Surely this is against the treaty?"

The Stone mage was of no further help to her. He didn't know the ins and outs of the Treaty of Swords. There was only one who might. Alena. She was a Sword who knew everything about the castle and everything under its roof. Surely Alena would know how the Serafina/Cole double act would affect the treaty and the kingdom? But what was the point of even wondering? Ember thought, trying to find a cool spot on her pillow. She couldn't get into the Swords' castle. Not now, not ever.

The light faded slowly, throwing long shadows across the room, and still she couldn't sleep. Her mind turned to Kalin, who had been so patient with her training, who had smiled and teased her as they danced, his blue eyes sparkling with affection. She had treated him abominably, and now he was probably dead, and Apoli had lost him forever. She was unaware of the tears pouring down her cheeks, and when she finally wiped them away, she wasn't sure if she was crying for Kalin, for Apoli, for Ashe, or herself.

CHAPTER 29

The commemoration was a blaze of Stones pageantry, with speeches and dedications to the fallen and honours given to the brave, and at the end, the Stone mage revealed a new garden replete with spring flowers: bluebells, jonquils and daffodils, which would bloom forever frost-free, no matter how inclement the weather.

Apoli spent the entire ceremony dissolved in tears, her pretty face swollen and red, for Kalin had fallen in battle, his body lost somewhere at the bottom of the gorge.

Ember stood at the rear, not knowing what to say or do. She'd been the recipient of many calculating glances and she supposed the story of Ashe shielding her from a barrage of arrows was doing the rounds. Some whispered that her influence over the Blade might mitigate the damage the Stones had created by preventing the Swords from joining the Seeds. Before, they had merely been disapproving observers. Now, they had shown their hand. The prospect of retribution suddenly seemed very real, and Sten put the villages and settlements on alert, and sent out dozens of firebirds to the borders.

When the ceremony was over, Ember joined the others in the procession past their majesties, to curtsey and bow and offer congratulations on a campaign well fought and won.

After she had bowed to Sten, she told him she was happy to join the guards on their patrols, if he liked. Many had died, and although their positions would be filled soon enough, her presence might come in handy in the meantime.

"It's spring. One of the most dangerous times in the mountains. Spring thaw can do unpredictable things. Avalanches, if we're lucky. What do you call a Sword in an avalanche?" Sten asked, his thick eyebrows raised in an expression of childlike glee.

"I don't know," Ember said. "What do you call a Sword in an avalanche?"

"Dead," Sten replied and guffawed loudly, making others turn to see what was so funny.

Ruby dug a finger into his side. "Hush. Look solemn."

Sten immediately coughed and wiped the amusement from his face. "Of course, of course. No, my dear," addressing Ember, "If you wish to join the guards, you may, but I'd rather you practised your archery first."

Ember flushed, remembering the arrow that hadn't even cleared the gorge, and moved off with the others, returning to her chamber to get dressed for the ball.

She was in a pensive mood, sitting quietly as her maid dressed her hair and made up her face. She was eager to go, be seen, and then leave early, for she didn't much feel like dancing tonight. Thoughts of Ashe still consumed her, made everything else seem trivial. His condition distressed her, and she kept turning it over and over in her mind, worrying at it like a cat with a ball of wool. She had no doubt that the two of them, Cole and Serafina, would eventually drain him dry. And then what? Neither had wanted to be the Blade. Serafina had chosen to die by her own hand rather than be imprisoned for the rest of her life. Cole had won the tournament and the contest, fair and square. In his mind, and in the eyes of the entire country, he did not deserve to be the Blade. Serafina and the Adjudicator had played him for a fool, had played the entire kingdom. And now they were also playing with the limits of what the treaty allowed. If the Treaty of Swords were dissolved, would Ashe then be free? And what would Serafina and Cole do?

She checked her appearance in the marble framed mirror. The balls in the Kingdom of Stones were far more rowdy than that of the Swords; no flimsy gowns, delicate sandals, and elaborate headpieces here. Besides, it was going to be held outside and one had to be prepared for the temperature to drop. With that in mind, she was dressed warmly in a dark blue woollen outfit, the only accession to elegance a nipped-in waist and tightly cut pants which showed off the long, lean muscles of her legs. Constant training over the past few months had trimmed down her figure, and she hadn't been that curvy to begin with, she thought ruefully. Still, training was a pleasure she hadn't expected to find. Back home, she'd shunned the gym, preferring to walk the city streets and explore the many parks, often hiking up the surrounding hills to get a glimpse of the sea.

Back home ...

She hadn't thought of home in a long while. Sometimes she felt it only existed in a dream, that here and now was the only place and time that mattered. How many years had passed on Earth? And what had happened to Earth during the border battle of the Seeds, Stones and Swords? It didn't bear thinking about. Perhaps, because they had fought in no-man's-land, where no kingdom ruled, there were no repercussions. Perhaps everyone back home was just going about their business, living their lives.

Or perhaps something catastrophic had happened.

She frowned, running her fingers restlessly through her hair. It was nearly down to her shoulders, and could use a cut. She asked the maid to plait her hair into two tight French braids, and then she tucked a few snowdaisies into the weave. The daisies reminded her of Radi, and she decided to visit her in the next few days, just to make sure she was well. Perhaps she would have forgiven Ember for not immediately taking her to the Shields.

Somehow, she doubted it.

When she was ready, she slipped out of her chamber and hastened through the palace, joining the throng of fae heading down to the lake. The atmosphere wasn't as boisterous or jovial as the other balls she'd been to. There was an air of solemnity and decorum that she rarely associated with a fae party, but all the ingredients for fun were there: the warm silken pavilions, skating on the frozen lake, dancing on the island in the centre, refreshments and music.

Ember wandered along the lakeside, wondering if she could be bothered getting skates on for a turn on the ice, when she spotted Apoli sitting alone under a silk tent, her lips stained blood red from the wine in her goblet. Ember settled next to her, accepting a mug of hot cider from a passing servant.

"I don't want to be here." Apoli's voice was slurred, her pupils dilated black, and Ember wondered if she'd taken another intoxicant besides the wine.

"You don't have to stay," Ember said. "It's been a hard day for everyone. You could rest."

"No, I couldn't. That's the point of being here. To commemorate their deaths and celebrate our lives."

"I'm going early," Ember said.

"No one cares what you do." Her tone was brackish, and she waved her goblet at Ember, sloshing liquid on the cushions. "Kalin did, though. He cared about you."

"I know. I just—"

"But you were in love with the Blade. I knew it the moment I saw you two together, that very first time you visited us. You ... glowed. Even when you were scowling at him. Something in you shone. And he shone too. Just a glimmer. He was good at hiding it."

Ember couldn't help an eager smile. "Do you think so?"

"They're saying he saved your life at the gorge. He turned his back on his own people for you."

Unexpectedly, a lump came into Ember's throat. "I don't know what to do, Apoli. I don't know how to help him. He can't live like that. It's not right."

"That's the way of the world though, isn't it? We're forced to accept what it gives us. We're stuck in the roles we were given. There's no way out for any of us." She gave Ember an appraising look over the wet rim of her goblet. "That's not the way of humans, is it? You can be whatever you want to be, if you have the skills and talent."

"And money," Ember said, drily. "And a fair amount of luck. But yes, I suppose, we can change our fortunes, to some extent."

"I never thought I'd be jealous of a human. But it's just so ... dismal ... to think I'm going to be here forever, trapped in the mountains, alone."

A tear slipped down her cheek. Ember didn't know what to say. She took Apoli's hand and squeezed it. "You're not alone."

"But I am trapped."

"You wouldn't want to be at the Swords. From what I hear, Serafina is draining the kingdom dry. And you wouldn't like the Seeds either. It's all jungle. Nothing like this."

Apoli sighed. "Shut up, Ember. Stop trying to make me feel better."

Ember pressed her lips together in exaggeration and turned to watch the skaters instead. Apoli drank with bitter silence, and eventually rose, swaying.

"I'm going to soak in the hot pools. Perhaps I can replace this mood with something a little more ... convivial."

"Well, be careful. Don't drown."

"If you say so." She wandered off, carelessly tossing her empty goblet into the snow, and disappeared into the crowd.

Ember felt the shift in tension well before the lightning came. One minute everything was normal and the next, all the fae had paused, the ground trembling underfoot, the pressure in the atmosphere intensifying, the air becoming thicker. Light flashed, outlining everything and everyone in a halo of sickly yellow. Several of the fae screamed. Skaters stumbled to the bank; wings spread to hasten their pace. At first, it looked as though nothing had changed. But something had—a group of newcomers on the bank in front of the royal pavilion, newcomers draped in red, surrounding a familiar figure.

Ember rose, her mug dropping to the cushions next to her, a stain of cider splashing the silk. This could not be in any way good.

The Adjudicator's voice rang out across the lake, his frigid tones weaving an enchantment so strong that Ember could feel it wrapping itself around her, preventing her from lifting a finger, from blinking an eyelash. Even her heart was struggling to maintain a rhythm.

"My words are law. My judgement is final."

The jurors swayed in unison. A soft hum came from them, a gentle weaving of their magic with the Adjudicators, strengthening his work.

She tried to gasp, to fill her lungs, but could only take in the briefest gasp of air, barely enough to keep her mind functioning. But there was something else in her too, something brash and innovative, something rebellious and adventurous. It was the same quality that had forced her ancestors from their humble beginnings in the sea to crawl onto the land and breathe, to bully the earth into a domain of their making. Being human was considered a weakness in this land of magic and wonder, but now it was a strength. She was aghast and furious at the audacity of this hideous ghoul to try and control her. She refused to let him. And her human blood agreed. It was just a shred, but it was enough.

Pulling all her strength together, she forced a shield, the thinnest of bubbles, hazy in places, the molecules barely connecting, but its fragility still lessened the impact of the Adjudicator's power. And as his power over her diminished, she made it stronger and stronger until it completely encased her, thick and unyielding. And to her surprise, she found she could block him out.

Slowly, she turned, so as not to attract attention. Everyone else was frozen in place, as if the water in their veins had iced over. Only she had the power to move ... but Ruby and Sten were moving, too. They were dragged out of their pavilion, waists thrust forward, the tips of their boots trailing on the ground, as if a lasso had wound itself around their torsos and was slowly and inexorably tugged by invisible hands.

They hadn't given up, though. Their hands were linked as they attempted to wrap themselves in light as they had at the battle of the bridge. But unlike then, the light came and went in fits and starts, flickering madly as if it were a faulty connection.

The Adjudicator motioned, and Sten and Ruby slid out onto the ice toward the island in the middle. In a flash of red, he was there to meet them, the centre of attention from all those on the surrounding banks.

Ember watched in horror. It was a tableau of vengeance, a chance for the Adjudicator to shame the One and Two in front of their people. It reminded her of the time he hung her in a cage over the dancers in the Swords' ballroom, merely to prove it was he who held power over everyone. And who was he? The King of Kings? It was he who should be shamed.

"Perhaps you misheard my instructions regarding the travelling between kingdoms. Let me reiterate. There shall be no collusion, no war, no disharmony. Esha shall be at peace. If you cannot agree, you will be replaced."

Ember could feel fury emanating from the watching fae, and yet none could do anything. She was the only one not trapped in a column of ice. And so she did the only thing she could.

She went into her mind.

CHAPTER 30

The only dragon she'd felt any connection with was Diamond, and it was the sort of bond that a human has with a dog; empathy, understanding, and communication that comes with months of training and living with one another. As she understood it, the dragon-riders had a telepathic communication with their chosen mounts, as complex and intricate as a spoken language. She had wondered why the dragons hadn't already arrived and quickly realised that the spell holding everyone immobile was essentially freezing their communications as well. After that business with Lakin in the throne room, the Adjudicator wasn't taking any chances.

Ember's mind was still her own, but unfortunately, she'd never used it to communicate with a dragon before. She wasn't even sure how. She closed her eyes and found the flexing muscle in her mind.

Lakin! Beni!

In her head, she was screaming, but there was no response. She tried again.

Lakin! Beni!

She repeated herself over and over, watching Sten and Ruby rise into the air, under the total command of the Adjudicator. He was jerking them back and forth now, watching with a thin smile as their heads lolled helplessly like saggy-necked puppets.

Lakin! Beni!

The chant became meditative. The flex became a door opening, and she glimpsed a gilded mass roiling on the other side. It coiled like a snake and rose, as if suddenly glimpsing the open doorway, and then it dived in a thin golden stream, wrapping itself around her brain, forcing into the connections and wirings in her head. There were places it couldn't reach, synapses that wouldn't fire, and she knew that was her humanity fighting against it. But there was enough thin gold wire that made sense, that she could understand and interpret. Language. The lilting words she heard Ashe and Serafina utter, the language of higher fae that had eluded her until now.

Lakin! Beni!

It wasn't her own language. It was theirs, slippery and seductive. At once she heard an answering voice that was not her own, a voice of roiling fire, deep and resonant, the rumble of volcanoes and that which lurked beneath the mantle of the earth.

Whoooo callllllls?

She didn't know the words to tell them it was her. All she could do was repeat their names, desperately, over and over. And then another word gently floated to the fore of her mind. Diamond's name, her true name, the name she should have known but never had the chance to learn.

Ethera.

In answer, there came a cry of terrible grief, of anguish laid bare. Ember's head jerked up. The cry wasn't inside her head. It was echoing around the lake, the clamour of wind in the mountains, the enchanted howling that could enrapture and enchant, and drive fae to mindless heroics of bravery and foolishness.

Dragonsong.

The Adjudicator heard it too. His wrinkled face creased in consternation and his hold over Sten and Ruby must have wavered, for the golden flickering light of the rulers became stable and strong. They sank lower, their feet touching the ice again. Sten's wings were trying to unfold from within him, the shadow of feathers slowly unfurling, as though they had been sketched in pencil, reminding Ember of the Temple of Shields she had once seen in the mist, there, but not there.

Another wave of power came from the Adjudicator, forcing Sten's wings to nothingness, and the light went out.

But again came dragonsong, louder now, and one by one the jurors sagged, some clamping their hands to their ears in a vain attempt to smother the cry. In the moonlit sky, a group of black dots, growing larger and larger, a steady thrumming of a staccato beat matching the dragonsong as mighty wings beat in unison.

The Adjudicator's mouth sagged. The enchantment holding Sten and Ruby fell away, and their light blazed bright, wings emerging in tandem. All the fae were moving now, heads turning, breath puffing in outraged clouds of steam. But the One and Two didn't use their power to subdue the Adjudicator. Instead, they flew toward the bank, and the skaters did too, all tripping over themselves in their haste to get to shore before the fleet arrived.

For one glorious moment, the dragons hovered around the lake, black silhouettes against the star-filled sky, their wings beating slowly in unison, eyes blazing, and a little voice inside Ember muttered unhelpfully, "I wish I could paint this."

The Adjudicator flung up a shield around himself, just as the dragons attacked. But as Sten once said, 'there's not much one can do against dragon fire', and he had spoken of just *one* dragon, not the entire fleet. Their fiery bellows of rage turned ice to water and water to steam. All saw the Adjudicator's shield crack and shatter within moments, and his robed form crumble to ash.

Steam rose, shielding the scene in a swirling white, and still the dragons breathed fire until the island was a charred smoking pit, the waters boiling in a fury, the cacophony of dragonsong risen to a deafening shriek.

All stood frozen, not by enchantment, but in disbelief and shock. It was Sten who broke the tableau, flying to the jurors like an avenging eagle, brandishing his sword. He swung once, twice, thrice, and bodies lay before him. Some tried to run but were quickly brought down by guards. Their hoods had fallen from their faces, their features finally discernible. They were little more than skeletons, waxen, yellow skin stretched tightly over bone, as though they had been dead a long time. A juror turned to face Ember as he fell, and she fancied she saw a smile creep to his lips, as though glad he had finally found his rest.

The dragons swallowed their fire. All was silent except for the languorous beating of wings. Lakin landed on the bank with an earth-shattering thud, while the rest of the fleet banked and flew back to the mountains with echoing cries of satisfaction.

Lakin swung his mighty head, chartreuse eyes scanning the bank, and then he saw her. Their eyes held, and she felt him in her head, his voice soft.

The work is done.

She could understand him, but she didn't yet have the words to reply, so she nodded and smiled, and he gave a huff through his nostrils, before turning his attention back to Sten, mewling like a baby and ducking his head for Sten to scratch him between his horns.

Another was also staring at her, watchful and solemn, and Ember swallowed, dropping her gaze. It was Ruby, and she did not look happy.

CHAPTER 31

Once again, Ember was summoned to stand in front of the One and Two. The enormous throne room was empty save for the guards on the doors, and as she approached the dais, her footsteps echoed off the marble surrounds. Ruby and Sten sat erect in silver crowns and formal robes, but their expressions were serene, not stern, and that gave Ember courage.

"Once again, Ember," said Ruby, "we are here because of you."

Ember frowned. Surely *she* was here because of *them?* But she tried to look agreeable. "Yes, Your Majesty."

Sten cut a sharp look at Ruby. "Yet this time, we have to thank you. Lakin told us how you screamed for them."

"Since when have you been able to speak their language?" Ruby enquired. "Only rulers and heirs can do so. Our dragon-riders have studied it for years, and it is still difficult for them. For you to do so should be impossible."

Ember's mind went blank. She couldn't tell them the truth, that she was an heir to the Kingdom of Shields. How safe would she be if she did? "I—I don't know. It just came to me. Perhaps because I'm a human?"

"You are an odd creature." Ruby's tone was harried. "I don't know what to do with you. I wanted to dispose of you much earlier, but Sten has always taken your side. I suppose I should be grateful to him." Her face softened as she looked at the king, her eyebrows arching with a seductive quality that made Sten shift in his chair. "For if it weren't for him, you would surely be dead by now. And if it weren't for you, we would most likely be at the bottom of the lake."

Not that there was much lake left. Most of it had boiled away, killing everything living within its depths. It would need to be re-filled, the island restored and a cleansing ritual conducted, but after the commemoration festivities, nobody had much of an appetite for ceremonies just yet.

Ruby was still speaking. "And so what do you request? We shall grant you one only."

Ember was taken aback. She hadn't been expecting a reward at all. There was only one thing she wanted, and she wasn't sure how they would receive it. "Anything?"

Ruby's eyes narrowed. "Do you doubt our word?"

"No! Of course not." Ruby might have mellowed, but she still didn't trust Ember, and to be honest, Ember thought, she didn't en-tirely blame her. She took a deep breath. "I have to get to the Kingdom of Swords."

Ruby and Sten blinked in unison. Ember hastened on, her words tumbling over one another, faster and faster.

"We lost so many good fae during the Battle of the Bridge. We cannot afford to lose any more. And Serafina doesn't care about her own people. She cares about power. She'll march again and again until the whole of Esha is tight in her grasp—or until her kingdom is dust. She doesn't care."

"Then let the Swords be dust." Sten's tone was airy. "Let them be as the Shields. Let them burn. The fleet will take care of them."

Ember bit her lip. "There are many good, kind, clever fae among the Swords. Thousands of innocents. Just as there were in the Shields. You fae, you're ... you live so long that the ephemeral notion of life just doesn't seem to occur to you. You hardly have any babies. There are so few children at court that when I see one, it's surprising. Your people cannot afford to just snuff out lives as though they mean nothing. Soon there'll be none of you left, and your world will be ruled by ... garakworms."

Sten gave a huff of amusement but his eyes were sombre. "You're saying that we're fools."

"I'm saying that life is precious. No matter whose life it is."

"And you're suggesting that we ask Serafina to lay down her ambition?" Ruby was caustic. "Is that what you ask of us? Should we send for a scribe and a firebird?"

Ember shook her head. "Not exactly. I think Cole and Serafina have broken the Treaty of Swords. I thought the Stone mage would know all about it, but he doesn't. But there's a fae who does. Alena. If I can get to her, she might help. If I can prove they've broken the treaty, we might be rid of Serafina forever."

Ruby leaned back in her seat and exchanged a wordless glance with Sten. "We cannot get you into the castle. The alliance between our kingdoms is well and truly severed."

"Although the Sword might be happy that the dragons blasted her jailer to cinders," observed Sten.

Ruby gave Ember a disapproving stare. "You're a ridiculous amount of trouble. Can't even make a simple request without turning the palace upside down. Why can't you ask for a diamond necklace? Or a handsome fae to warm your bed at night?"

"Because they're hurting the Blade," Ember blurted. "They're killing him, not himself, but his mind, his inner essence. He's trying to stand up to them, but ... once he is gone, they will have his body to wield, and he will be terrible and mighty, and no one will stand in his way. I can't let them do that to him. I can't let him destroy the country for her. Please help me."

Tears stood in her eyes, and she swiped at them impatiently.

Ruby crowed with delight. "I knew it. I knew there was something between you."

"We all knew it," said Sten. "And finally, she does too."

"It took time," Ember allowed. "Too long. And time is running out for him. He's so weak, so ill ..."

Ruby frowned. "He looked well enough to me at the Battle of the Bridge."

Ember felt a flush warm her cheeks. "He wasn't himself." She hoped Ruby would take her word for it. She didn't want to be tied up in any truth ribbons and forced to answer awkward questions about her strange ability to get inside the pendant. Skirting around the truth of the fae language had been hard enough.

"I liked Ashe once," Ruby said. "But I shall never forgive him for what he has done."

"It wasn't him," Ember said. "That's not who he is. He is hers to wield."

Ruby slowly shook her head, and in that moment, Ember knew she was going to refuse. She threw herself on her knees. She'd never begged for anything before, and it humiliated her, but she couldn't think of anything else.

"Please, please. I just need to get to the border."

"You did promise," Sten remarked, and Ruby sighed.

"Then so shall it be. We shall use shadowing to get you to the border, but you must make your way through on foot. You may take whoever you like. But if you are caught, we shall deny any involvement. We must remain apart from these troubles and keep our people safe. We will take a lesson from the Skies and lock down."

"We'll talk about that," Sten said to her in a low voice, and she nodded.

"Thank you." Ember rose, her mind racing. She would visit Radi and ask the Stone mage if there was an easier way to get out of the mountains than shadowing. Some things were much better in Esha, she thought as she hurried from the throne room, but what wouldn't she give for a beat-up old car?

CHAPTER 32

R ecalling the hardships she'd endured on her own in a hostile land, she decided to take two guards with whom she had trained before: Wharaki, an excellent hunter and tracker, and Pena, who was renowned for his bravery and fighting skills. They leapt at the chance for adventure, and the possibility of putting one over the Swords. Both had lost friends at the Battle of the Bridge, and both wanted revenge. Ember had told them several times their mission was to get in, learn what they could, and get out again, but she knew they would be glad for a reason to fight.

The maid equipped her for her journey—Ember particularly insistent on having her warm travelling cloak resewn with several deep pockets, which her last one had been sorely lacking in—and she had an arsenal of knives, a slingshot, and her spear, foregoing the bow entirely, her inadequacy at the bridge proving that carrying it was likely more of a hindrance than anything else. She made sure she had a potion to repel insects (particularly effective against badgebugs, the healer assured her), adequate rations and a supply of hooks and lines for fishing. She also took a few crash lessons in snaring small animals and foraging for food. Hunger was not something she wished to repeat.

She and the guards set off to the Stone mage's cottage at dawn. The sky was leaden grey with a tinge of rosy pink, which promised a fine day. Snowdaisies bloomed cheerfully along the track, and curious, Ember put one in her mouth and chewed it, wondering if Radi had liked the bitter taste. Likely, she had been so hungry that being choosy wasn't an option.

They were barely out of the palace grounds, just at the foot of the winding path into the hills, when they heard running footsteps and a breathless, "Hey! Wait!"

The trio turned to see Apoli hurrying toward them, pack on her back, long hair fluttering in the breeze. "I'm coming too."

Ember was taken aback. "We're not going on a picnic. You can't come."

"But—"

Ember cut her off. "Does the queen know you're here?"

"Not exactly."

"Which means no. You don't have permission and I'm not putting the queen's niece in danger. She'd blast me to dust in a second if anything happened to you."

"Well, if anything *did* happen to me, it would probably have happened to you, too. She can't blast you to dust if you're already dead."

Ember sighed in exasperation. "I can't look after you. And these two? They're looking after me."

"So I'm on my own. I don't care. I'm coming." Her voice became wheedling as she changed tack. "Please, Ember. I want to see some of the world before I die. And I want to do something that matters."

Ember tried to cut in, but Apoli raised her voice.

"Kalin died defending his kingdom. He was noble and good and sacrificed himself without fear of death. I want to live up to his memory. I want him to be proud of me. The One and Two will lock down the kingdom, and I'll never be able to go anywhere ever again." Her eyes grew glossy, but she blinked back the unshed tears. "Please, Ember."

Ember sighed. "I'm sure Kalin is proud of you. Look—you can come as far as the mage's cottage, alright? But then you'll have to go back."

Apoli scowled, but attempted to force her face into agreeable lines. "Of course." And then flashing the guards a flirtatious smile, "Hello, boys."

Ember rolled her eyes. "Apoli. We don't have time for any of that."

She started back up the path, the guards falling into step with her, and she pretended not to hear Apoli saying lightly, "Oh, there's always time for *that*."

They moved at a relatively quick pace, but although Apoli was in perfect health, she'd never really done much in the way of exercise, and was soon puffing and blowing. Ember and the guards carried on ahead, leaving her to catch up. Ember half-hoping if Apoli found it hard going now, she'd decide she wouldn't be able to keep up if trekking through the Kingdom of Swords, and had better go home.

But Apoli proved to be of stronger stuff than Ember imagined, and she didn't voice a single complaint, or ask for extra rest. She just ploughed on stoically, her eyes fixed on the trail, ignoring the expansive view of the mountains, her thoughts clearly far, far away from there.

Eventually they halted for a break, and rather than break into their rations too soon, they cooked an unlucky rabbit Wharaki had shot on the way. Its white fur was turning to brown as the season changed, and the pale head, in contrast to the rest of its body, looked as though it had face-planted in a tin of white paint. It was lean from winter, and there was only enough for a few bites each, but the gamey meat was hot and delicious, and they chased it down with a handful of spring flowers Ember had learned were edible: snowdaisies, dandelions and violets, which Apoli chewed for a microsecond before spitting out her mouthful in disgust.

Soon, the mage's cottage came into view. Ember cast an uneasy glance upward just in case the mage had taken his other form, but the skies were empty. As they approached the footbridge, the cottage door banged open and Radi burst out.

"Wait here," Ember said to the others hastily and darted over the bridge, hoping Radi wouldn't yell out "my queen" or anything else she would have to explain.

"Who's that?" Apoli said, just as Radi flung herself into Ember's arms, her face alight.

Ember pushed her away to look at her. The days spent with the mage had been good for her. She looked well rested, there was colour in her cheeks, and the gaunt cast to her features had vanished.

"Who's that?" she said, peering over her shoulder at Apoli and the guards.

"No one. Listen," Ember said in an undertone. "Don't tell them who you are. And don't tell them who I am either."

Radi frowned. "Why?"

The mage appeared in the doorway, and Ember waved a hand in greeting. The guards, however, sank into deep bows and Apoli swept a low curtsey, which would have looked much better if she'd been wearing a skirt. All looked decidedly uncomfortable. The mage inspired awe in others, even if Ember saw him as more of a friend.

The mage didn't invite them in, merely telling Radi to go back to the house. She did so with an ill-grace; the door slamming in pique behind her.

"The Adjudicator overreached himself, I hear. And the Swords now prepare to march, not to the Seeds," he said, forestalling Ember's query, "but to the grasslands. They're set on taking the centaurs' lands for their own, and then they'll march on. Serafina has been unleashed. There is no one to restrain her, and she is hungry."

"I need to get to Alena. If she can help me, then perhaps we can end this before it starts. Can you help us, please? I can't do shadowing, I just can't. It nearly suffocated me last time, even with Xarin at my side."

Apoli snorted in derision. "You should see the rock she tried to sculpt," and then, as if remembering to whom she was speaking, fell silent, pretending to be very interested in the gravel at her feet.

The mage tilted his head as he studied Ember, and he smiled. "Then perhaps you'd better climb aboard."

Chapter 33

F lying through the mountains on the mage's dragon form was exhilarating. He had no saddles or handholds, and they had to clutch his scaly spines and cling on as best they could, but the view and speed made up for the uncomfortable ride.

The mage had allowed Radi to come, and her squeals of delight rang out in a merry peal as they soared over the frozen landscape. The mage told Radi this was just a one-off trip for her, and she would return with him. She readily agreed, so taken with the idea of riding a dragon, she would have happily agreed to anything.

Apoli had told Ember vehemently that she wasn't going back to the palace, and if Ember didn't let her come, she would open out her veins and bleed to death in front of them all. Ember replied sharply that she didn't take well to blackmail and handed Apoli a dagger, whereupon Apoli flung it on the ground in a fit of temper, shouting that Ember had no right to stop her from going anywhere because she, Ember, was only a stupid human and she, Apoli, was of royal blood. It threatened to get very ugly until the mage stepped in, telling Apoli that he would smooth things over with the One and Two himself.

Apoli, good humour restored, returned Ember's dagger with a gracious apology and a promise not to make any more trouble. Ember couldn't even be bothered being angry with her. Her only thought, her every fibre in her being, was singing with one word.

Ashe.

As they flew over the Stones' territory, the mage spoke to them in their heads, pointing out the landmarks: Mount Fronian, where gold and diamonds were mined, the Ketra Ranges, home to the very first One and Two, and the Hydra Gully, where mustada lived, a type of ice dragon that breathed not fire, but a toxic gas that would cause a fae to lose their senses and die, if they weren't treated in time. They weren't large creatures, barely knee-high, but they hunted in packs and could easily take down animals much larger than themselves. Ice statues of fae stood at the perimeter of nearby villages to confuse the herds and keep them busy long enough to be taken down by spears.

To their left, beyond the granite mountains, lay the domain of the Shields, an expanse of undulating dirt and rocks, as far as the eye could see. And yet, she thought, she glimpsed something gleaming in the distance. Water. And edging it, a faint hint of green. Looking at it made her feel peculiar, as if a thread was pulling her upright, straightening her spine. Blood churned inside her veins, and a surge of sentiment welled up inside her, of pride, nostalgia and love. The mage's scaly skin rippled, as sensing the emotion within her, and his voice spoke inside her mind.

"Not yet."

He banked sharply so the Kingdom of Shields disappeared behind them, and made Apoli shriek with fright, her voice stolen by the wind.

The closer to the Swords they got, the stronger was Ember's sense of foreboding. She closed her eyes and tried to reach out to Ashe, tried to unlock the magic that came unbidden when she was full of terror, the power that allowed her to step inside his mansion, but there was nothing, not even a closed door to bang against.

The snowy mountains gave way to rugged hills, and then the dark green of the outer forests. Ahead lay the land of the Swords, that placid, rich countryside of gentle rolling pasture. The castle lay somewhere ahead, hidden by distance, but just the thought of those grey stones and black turrets was enough to send a shiver down her spine.

They landed in a clearing among the pine trees, the wide strip of the border just ahead cutting through the forest. Clumps of snow still dotted the ground, but the climate was far milder than that of the mountains. All was quiet.

The travellers slid from the mage's back, Ember stumbling as she hit the ground, her arms and thighs trembling with the strain of holding on. The mage turned his huge blue head to lock eyes with her.

"I wish you good fortune," came the voice in her head, and she replied in kind.

"Thank you."

"And, er ..." His voice came in a rush, "You might bid Alena good day. From me."

Ember hid her smile, but her eyes danced. "Of course." She spoke out loud. "Goodbye Radi. I'll see you soon." She didn't add, "I hope."

Radi, still sitting on the mage's back, just waved nonchalantly, apparently not seeing any reason Ember shouldn't. "Bye, Ember," and then to the mage, "Can we take the long way home?"

217

The mage took a few running steps before launching into the air, his wings straining to make height, the immense body only just scaling the trees on the other side of the clearing. He circled once, and flew back toward the hills, leaving them alone.

The others looked at Ember expectantly, and she, suddenly realising she was the leader now, said, "If we can find a river nearby, we can call Alena, but otherwise, we'll have to travel to a village called Greyclare. A friend lives there, who can summon her—I mean, request her to come."

Wharaki retrieved a cloth map from his pack and unrolled it, spreading it on the grass. They crouched around it as he jabbed at a dark green splodge on the map. "We're here. The nearest river isn't far. But your Greyclare lies on the far side of the kingdom."

Ember gazed in dismay at the map. She knew it was a long way, but not that far.

Apoli was staring too, not at the map, but at Wharaki. "I thought you were supposed to be some kind of amazing tracker? Why did you bring a map? Can't you just sense your way?"

"I brought it for my lady," he said shortly, turning to Ember and bowing. "*She* can read a map."

The implication was that Apoli couldn't, and Ember turned away to hide her amusement. Apoli was about to get a very sharp lesson in real life, and her performance earlier with the dagger hadn't exactly endeared her to her companions. Wharaki and Pena were the best in their field, and neither suffered fools, no matter what their title. Ember had trained under both of them, and although her skills were lacking, she made up for it with sheer doggedness, often the first to training sessions and the last to leave, and she made a point of never complaining, no matter how tired she was. They held a measure of respect for her, but Apoli had yet to earn theirs.

"Then we had best make tracks," she said, to cover the awkward silence. It was already afternoon and they would be lucky to reach the river by dark. Wharaki led the way through the clearing and as they reached the line of the border, Apoli's eyes glittered with excitement.

"I've never been out of the kingdom before." She gasped in wonder as they entered the strange sepia world of no-man's-land. "How gloomy the Swords is! You never said."

Ember smiled. "It's just the border. It's brighter on the other side."

"Shhh," Pena cautioned them, his finger to his lips, and the others fell silent.

The border cut through the trees as if it were a brown crayon. Scrubby bushes and yellow grass sprouting from cracked grey earth lay within, as if the border had sucked not only the colour out of the forest, but the life as well. It felt different to the border she had fought in between the Swords and the Seeds. This place was eerie, unwelcoming. The wind rushed through the long grass stalks, setting them waving restlessly, but when Ember listened carefully, it was as though a mournful voice carried on the rushing gusts.

A life half-lived is a life half-died ... A half-life lived is a half-life died ...

Th monotonous refrain continued as she walked, and she wondered what it meant. Something like the saying about the optimist's glass being half full, she supposed. A nervous muscle jumped in Wharaki's jaw, and Pena's knuckles were white on his spear. Apoli had her hands clamped over her ears. All three looked to be suffering migraines, but the whispering didn't affect Ember at all. It was just annoying.

She cast a shield around them, and they relaxed, continuing on with a renewed determination, breaking into a half-trot as they reached the edge. When they emerged on the other side to the embrace of the bright, warm light of the Swords, Apoli turned to Ember.

"Was that you?"

Ember drew her shield back into herself and nodded. "You looked in pain."

"Could you not feel them?"

"Them?"

"The spirits of the dead, wandering through the borderlands."

"I heard a whisper. I just thought it was the wind."

Pena shuddered. "That's what happens to fae who do not live their lives as they should. Their energy is confined to this plane, doomed."

"Oh." Ember said, and then, recalling Radi's talk of the spirits who liked to steal one's breath, said, "Is that like snow spirits?"

All three exchanged glances, eyes wide. "Quiet, my lady. It's best not to talk of such things," said Wharaki. "It's bad luck."

Ember frowned. Radi had spoken of them willingly enough. Perhaps it was just the Stones who didn't like the snow spirits.

The forest was different on the Swords' side. Warmer, for one thing, with lush green trees as opposed to the snowy pines just a few paces north. Apoli was in a paroxysm of delight, turning her face to the sun, and declaring dramatically that she was far too warm for her outer tunic as she slipped it off and wrapped it around her waist. Almost immediately they scared up a flock of fat partridges which Wharaki shot on the wing, tying a brace together to hang off his pack until they could make camp for the evening.

It was a pleasant hike. Ember had to remind herself she was in enemy territory now and conjured another shield to muffle their footsteps. Although they were in the outer forest far from villages, there might still be bandits or hunters, or breeds of fae that shunned civility, preferring to live wild. And, of course, there were predators as well. It wasn't long before they heard foliage rustling and a high-pitched squeal as the shadow of something swung through the tree branches toward them.

CHAPTER 34

Pena drew his bow in an instant. He rapid-fired arrows at the shadowy thing leaping from branch to branch, but missed every time as the thing folded and refolded in on itself, its legs shrinking and lengthening to avoid the shafts whizzing through the air.

"It's a darkling," Wharaki said. He didn't look particularly worried, and that gave Ember some comfort, although not Apoli, who shivered and whimpered, her fingers in a death grip on Ember's arm. "It's not venomous. It'll just take chunks out of you."

"Oh, that's good, then," said Ember drily, as an arrow finally pierced the thing's pointed head. With a splash of black blood, it howled and fell off the branch it was clinging to, its many legs drawing in on itself as it crashed to the ground, reminding Ember of a spider hit with fly spray.

Wharaki showed her how thin its torso was, barely thicker than a sheet of cardboard, so it could effortlessly bend itself in midair. Ember stroked the fibres of its leathery skin. It was unexpectedly soft and luxuriant.

"Some use its skin for furnishings." Wharaki said. "Stretch it across a frame for a seat, or sew it for cushions and the like."

"I might take it back with me," said Apoli. "It'll be a souvenir."

"You'll have to peel it and scrape it," said Wharaki. "It'll stink otherwise."

She gave him a sideways glance, a lift of a pointed eyebrow. "Then that's what I shall do."

Wharaki gave a disbelieving snort, and Apoli's eyes narrowed. Ember and Pena exchanged a glance, and Ember said hastily, "Well, shall we make camp then? We might as well. It'll be dark soon."

They set up around a campfire, which Wharaki had dug in a trench, so they could cook their food without too much firelight giving them away. While Apoli wrestled with her darkling, exchanging barbed comments with Wharaki who was prepping the two partridges with Ember's help, Pena prowled around the perimeter, restlessly scanning the area, but all was quiet.

Apoli finally finished scraping her skin and hung it up over the bushes to dry before burying the head and guts of it. She wanted to wash her hands, but Wharaki flatly refused to let her use their drinking water, and so she had to scrub her hands with leaves, muttering darkly under her breath.

They ate the cooked birds in silence. Ember was too preoccupied with thoughts of Ashe to notice the glares exchanged between Apoli and Wharaki, and Pena was too much of a warrior to betray their position with idle chitchat. They cast the bones in the fire before covering it over and then turned in, each with their backs to each other.

Sleep came easy for Ember that night. She'd only just closed her eyes, and then she was inside the mansion. Ashe lay on the couch, his skin tinged with grey, the colour a very old person has before they die. With effort, he turned to look at her and his eyes grew soft.

"Ember." He attempted to rise, but she put out a hand and bade him lie still.

"What did they do to you?"

"She was very angry."

"It's not just her. It's Cole as well."

He looked as though he was trying to understand. "Cole?"

"They're ... sharing the same body. That's why you're so sick. They're sucking you dry."

Relief flitted across his face, and for an instant, the swirling of colours beneath his skin rose to the brown surface before sinking again. "Of course. How could I have not known?"

"They're being clever. I don't think anyone knows. But I might be able to help. You just have to hold on a little longer. You cannot let them win. If your spirit dies, they will still have your body to use. And if your body dies, then I imagine Cole will become the Blade. Serafina is stronger than he is."

He nodded, and with a swift movement, took her hand and squeezed it. "I wish this wasn't a dream. I wish this were real." She blinked in genuine confusion, but he was still talking, as if to himself. "For if it were real, I would remind you of the first time I saw you. Do you remember? You were terrified of me. And then the next time, at the castle, you shouted at me."

He laughed softly, and a warm light came into his eyes. "One foot in fae and already you were finding yourself. And now ... you're so beautiful and strong. And I love to see it. I love dreaming of you. I have to keep telling myself to wake, or else I would stay in the dream of you forever." His voice faded, and he tugged her closer. "I don't want to wake up. Please, my darling, stay with me a little longer."

She breathed him in, felt the warmth of him against her skin. Just to be next to him was enthralling, intoxicating, and with a heated rush, she remembered the writhing, passionate afternoon they'd spent in the clouds when he'd told her it was just once, only once.

He narrowed his eyes, as if he knew exactly what she was thinking, and the tip of his tongue came out to wet his lips. Deliberately, she placed a hand on his thigh and leaned in closer.

"It's just a dream," she told him, and kissed him lightly, her tongue flicking out to lick his lower lip. "Just a dream."

He opened his mouth and his arms tightened around her, pulling her in toward him, his lips hungrily taking hers. She moaned against his mouth as he untied the leather fastenings at her throat, slipping a hand inside her top to caress her breasts. Her nipples hardened as he brushed his knuckles against them, and suddenly he flipped her, bending her back over the couch, sucking at her bare breasts while she arched under him.

Her own hands were busy stroking his cock beneath his pants, straining against the enclosing fabric, and he groaned. All at once he was naked, while she was clad in a black bikini, the one he had dressed her in when they escaped to the beach for one long afternoon.

She smiled at him, her breath hitching. "You like this one?"

"If you knew," he growled, one hand pulling aside fabric so he could slide a finger into her wetness, "how much I wanted you that day ..." he withdrew his finger and licked it, tasting her juice with evident pleasure, and then yanking down the fabric altogether so that he could slowly slide two fingers into her. "But you were so drained. A shadow of who you were. If I tried to seduce you, I would have scared you back into his arms. So I waited. To make you feel safe."

"If I remember correctly, you fell asleep," she pointed out, clenching his shoulders as he withdrew his hand, added another finger.

"Perhaps I felt safe too," he murmured, biting the soft skin on her neck, and she shivered. The girth of his three fingers in her was delicious, and she rocked against his hand as he pushed in deeper, a wet thumb circling her clit. He knew exactly what to do to get her off, knew exactly how much she loved this pleasurable pain, and as he placed his other hand around her throat, her eyes widened with anticipation. He squeezed, his voice hissing through his teeth.

"I wanted to own you. I wanted to keep you, just like he did."

He leaned over and bit her nipples through the black bikini top and she bucked, moaning his name. She was imprisoned in his grip while his clever thumb rubbed and flicked, her pussy straining against his fingers. Just a little more, and she would shatter, just a little more ...

The hand around her neck slid away, and she mewed in disappointment and frustration.

He smiled, his dark eyes glittering. "The only difference is, I didn't."

"The difference is, I'm here because I want to be, not because I have no choice," she replied.

Slowly, he withdrew his hand, and she quickly sat up and leaned forward, capturing his cock in her mouth. He gave an approving growl as she licked and sucked, taking him in as far as she could, one hand around the base, twisting and pumping. He placed a hand on her scalp and forced her head down, lower. The tip of his cock rammed against the back of her throat and she hummed, saliva dripping down onto her hand. He jerked his hand away, but she snatched at it, drawing it back to her hair, and he, understanding her need to be dominated, forced her head down again.

"Good girl," he told her approvingly, and she choked and swallowed, her throat wide. Her hand crept up to stroke his balls, and she felt him stiffen.

She pulled her head back. "You like that?"

"Who the fuck told you to stop?" He wound his fingers in her hair and forced her back down again and she hummed around his cock, one hand working his shaft, the other stroking and caressing his balls, until he was groaning and thrusting up toward her. Her desire bloomed anew at his obvious pleasure in her skills, in his need for her. She could feel her pussy dripping wet, swollen from his fingers and tongue, now forlorn and under-appreciated. His fingers found her mouth, stretched wide around his girth, before sliding back to her hair, and he yanked her upright.

The jerk on her scalp sent another arrow of pleasure through her, and she licked her swollen lips, smiling with seductive promise. A black fog had filled the room, a fog of lust and passion and incomplete desire. He was studying her, his dark eyes glittering.

"Bend over. Hurry."

She obeyed, her muscles already clenching at the thought of him inside her. She leaned her forehead against the arm of the couch and moaned as his breath whispered against her hot wetness. He devoured her then, his fingers and mouth all over her, licking her pussy, sliding inside, up to her anus, interspersing his caresses with stinging slaps that made her squeal and writhe.

"Please," she moaned. "Please ..."

"Please, what?"

"Please fuck me."

She thought he might delay, might wring out the sweet torment a little longer, but he couldn't wait. He forced his cock into her, slow and deep, and then withdrew, almost to the tip. She backed up to meet him, and he slammed into her, hard and fast. He slid a hand into her hair, pulling her head back and they came together in a violent rush, the echoes of her cries mingled with his.

They lay entwined on the couch, in a half-doze of satisfaction, a sheen of sweat clinging to their skins. She stirred to look at him. His eyes were closed, but as she moved, he opened them, seemingly surprised to see her there.

"Ember?"

The room shuddered and the lace panels covering the windows fell, shattering on the floor. The table skidded across the room, and the chandelier jerked back and forth.

"Is it an earthquake?" she cried.

"You have to leave, Ember." A rumbling noise, like a freight train approaching, grew louder and louder. "I have to wake up."

"What?"

"Wake up!"

Pena was shaking her awake. The dark of night still clung to the world, and it was her turn to keep watch. Pena settled in her place to catch a couple of hours of sleep, while she sat with her back to a tree with her dagger in her hand and her spear within easy reach. Her blood still fizzed with the memory of Ashe's touch, but she was overcome with foreboding. What was happening at the mansion? What was happening with Ashe?

The grey light of dawn soon came. She woke the others, and they moved off into the forest.

CHAPTER 35

S he mistook the rushing of the current through the trees for the wind at first. But as they drew closer, shimmering waters reflected the light, casting strange rippling beams across the trees. It wasn't so much a river as a fast-flowing, shallow stream, and she wondered how Alena would swim along it, assuming that she could even hear Ember calling her. They were a long way from the castle, a long way from anywhere. If Alena didn't come, they'd have to hike to Greyclare and how long would it take before Serafina realised intruders were in her kingdom?

Wharaki, Pena, and Apoli watched expectantly as Ember scrambled down the bank to the stream and hunkered down on her heels to dabble her hand in the water.

"Alena!"

The only reply was the water gurgling over rocks.

"Alena! It's Ember." She glanced up at the others with a crooked smile. "I'm not sure what to do."

She'd expected Apoli to make a caustic remark about her lack of magical talent, but Apoli said helpfully, "Don't just use your voice. Use your mind too."

Ember nodded. She dipped her hand in the water again, letting the cool liquid bubble over her fingers. She closed her eyes and focused. "Alena!" Her mind's voice had taken on a strange muted quality, as though she were screaming underwater. She called the forest fae's name, over and over, but there was nothing, no sense of her.

She sat back on her haunches and sighed, flicked the water from her fingers. "Maybe I'm doing it wrong."

"Then we had best make haste to your Greyclare," Wharaki said. "It will be many days."

"We don't have many days," Ember said bleakly, recalling Ashe and the way he had looked when she'd sat with him, so drawn and ill. Not so much afterwards, she thought with a flush of heat to her cheeks and suddenly she wondered if perhaps she had given him some kind of human strength, had fed him with her essence the way Cole had so often drawn from hers. Perhaps that might be enough to sustain him against the two who drained him, at least long enough for them to reach Greyclare.

She scrambled up the bank, reaching for Pena's hand to pull her up, when there came a bubbling and boiling behind her, a geyser containing far more water than the stream could have provided. A familiar figure emerged from the gushing waters, her silver hair perfectly coiffed, her green dress shimmering around her. As she stepped onto the grass, the geyser collapsed, sending a wave of water downstream.

"Goodness, child. You do get yourself into the most ridiculous situations."

"Alena!" Ember slid down the bank and made to hug Alena.

The fae hurriedly backed off, her hands up. "You're filthy."

"Sorry." Ember grinned at her, aware that she had missed Alena more than she had realised. "How are you?"

Alena shrugged airily. "Well enough. Who are they?"

"These are my travelling companions, Wharaki, Apoli and Pena."

Pena and Wharaki bowed, and Apoli swept her curtsey.

Alena studied her, eyes narrowed. "She's of the Stones court, I take it? Do they all look like that?"

"Like what, exactly?" said Apoli icily.

Ember frowned at her. She couldn't afford for Alena to take offence and vanish.

"As though you've been on a hunt for a week. Although I suppose you curtsey well enough."

Apoli pressed her lips together as if smothering a retort and inclined her head gracefully.

"Alena," Ember said. "I need to know about the Treaty of Swords. I think it's been broken."

Alena shook her head. "Impossible, or we'd all know about it." A wicked gleam came into her eyes. "Just as we all know about the Stones' dragons murdering the Adjudicator. What a triumph for the Stones! The Sword was beside herself with delight. The festivities went on, night and day, for a week. I suppose that's the only reason she's marching on the dear centaurs rather than yourselves. Although I can't imagine that peace will last. She's not forgiven you for the Battle of the Bridge, much less the Blade, who unfortunately had to bear her rage alone. Lucky for the rest of us, I suppose."

"Surely the treaty states that there can be only one Sword and one Blade?" said Ember.

"Of course."

"But there's not! There's *two* Swords. Cole and Serafina are sharing one body. He didn't go anywhere. He's there with her. And they're draining the Blade dry."

Alena's eyes widened, and her mouth sagged. It was the first time Ember had seen her so discomposed, and she fancied she saw the flicker of scaly skin pushing itself against the surface of Alena's smooth cheek, before sinking away again.

"That cannot be true. For you are correct. The treaty would break. Unless they're replacing one another, rather than sharing. Switching so quickly that only one occupies the body at a time, rather than two sharing and each coming forth when they choose."

"But ... where does the other one go?"

Alena shrugged. "Likely a place between worlds. You passed through one between Earth and Esha. Now, was that all?"

Ember dropped her head, defeated. She was so sure the treaty would break once the truth of Serafina and Cole was revealed, but they had found a loophole. And soon Ashe, the Ashe she loved, would be no more.

"There's another thing." Ember glanced up at the others and lowered her voice. "I've discovered more about my fae side. I'm a Shield. The daughter of an heir. And—"

Alena reared back, her green skirts rippling in a non-existent breeze and then she transformed, swelling and expanding, her serene face splitting and falling away to reveal a long jutting snout, lizard-like eyes, green bubbled skin, tail restlessly smacking the water. She was a crocodile creature on two legs, her true form, the one Ember had only caught glimpses of until now.

"You're *what?*" Alena roared. She started toward Ember, who hastily stumbled back, tripped, and ended up sprawled on the muddy bank.

Both Pena and Wharaki drew their bows, and Apoli shouted, "Ember, you dozy twit—what did you say to her?"

Feet skating in the mud, Ember struggled to her feet, refusing to be cowed. "It's true. I knew it as soon as they told me."

"Who told you?"

"Another Shield. And then the Stone mage confirmed it."

"The mage?" Alena's skin rippled, and she seemed to shrink a little. She turned away, muttering, "Can it be true? The girl has always been hard to read—but surely the human side of her—although she withstood the heir's attentions better than most ..."

She was speaking to herself in a rapid undertone, interspersed with growls and the occasional smack of her tail, and Ember wasn't sure if she should interrupt or not.

"What is she talking about?" Apoli hissed. "What did you do?"

Ember sighed. What did it matter if anyone else knew now? "I'm a Shield."

The look on their faces would have been funny, but she was too preoccupied with Alena, who was now marching back and forth in the stream, kicking up sprays of water, gesticulating wildly, her hands—or rather, claws—clicking together convulsively.

Finally, she whipped around to face them. Ember squeezed her eyes shut, waiting for Alena to blast her to a puddle, for after all, Alena was a Sword, and she was a Shield, an enemy. But nothing happened. When she cautiously opened her eyes again, the reptilian figure had dissolved into the elegant woman Ember knew.

"Your Majesty," Alena said, and inclined her head.

Wharaki and Pena exchanged incredulous glances. Apoli's face paled. "What the fu—"

"The double act of the Sword shall not break the treaty," Alena said. "It shall never be so."

Ember sagged, her last hope dashed.

But Alena was still speaking. "The only thing that can break the treaty … is you."

CHAPTER 36

"But ... if that were true, wouldn't the treaty already know I existed, that I was here?" Ember said.

"Obviously not," said Alena. "I imagine your humanity is blocking the way. It needs your blood."

"My... blood?"

"The Treaty of Swords stands because the Shields don't exist, because their line was well and truly done. The Shields title is hereditary, unlike the Skies, who elect their leaders, and the Stones who are chosen by dragons. Only blood will prove your right to rule. Dissolve the treaty and the Blade shall no longer be confined. He will be free."

"Yes," said Ember. "That's what he deserves."

"And then there will be three Swords' rulers roaming around. Three of them! Each powerful and vengeful ... and perhaps united."

Ember shook her head, "No. Serafina took the title of Sword away from Cole. I can't imagine he's happy about that. And Ashe wants to be free of them. They aren't united."

And yet, a nagging fear nudged at her. What if they were? Two had destroyed the Shields, razed it to a wasteland of dirt and rock. What could three do?

No, she replied to herself. That won't happen. That can't happen. Ashe would not allow it.

But he's so weak ... could he resist them combined?

Stop it.

"Then blood it must have," she said, trying to inject a note of determination into her voice, but it didn't sound very convincing.

"Even then, it might not be enough. It will have to see through your humanity. Besides, the Sword will discover you are here as you advance to the heart of the kingdom, if she does not know already. You must shield yourself from her ..." She broke off and turned away with a wry chuckle. "Why am I even helping you? I betray my kingdom just by being here."

"No, you're not. You're helping to save your kingdom. You're helping to save Esha."

"Good. Pray tell the Sword before she decides to lop off my head," Alena said drily.

Ember smiled and turned back to practicalities. "It will take us days to get to Riverburn. Can you help us?"

"I can help you, but not them. They'd sink. Like Stones." She smiled at her own cleverness, but Ember didn't.

"But ... how can I do this alone? If she knows I'm here, I'll have no one to defend me."

"Such is the price of heroics. The greatest things we do, we do alone."

Ember bit her lip. "Would you excuse me for just a moment?"

"Why yes, for I have nothing else to do but to wait on you."

Ignoring the sarcasm, Ember scrambled back up the bank and faced the others. "I must go on alone. But I thank you for your companionship. I'm sorry it wasn't much more of an adventure than this. If you return to the clearing, and call the Stone mage, I'm sure he will return for you."

The two warriors bowed, accepting their orders with equanimity, but Apoli pouted. "You're cutting short our trip?"

"It's not a holiday!" Ember said. "You're not even supposed to be here!"

"Well, I'm not going back," she replied mutinously. "I've only just left."

Ember gave a helpless shrug. "Then do not. Explore the world. Do what you must. As I do what I must."

"Really?" Apoli's face lit up.

"You're an adult. And I don't have time to argue with you."

She kissed Apoli on the cheek and held out her hand to Wharaki to shake. He stared at her hand in bewilderment, and Ember dropped it. "Never mind."

Handing her pack to Pena, she addressed the two warriors. "If you want to look after Apoli, you may. And if you don't, you must return home. Do what your conscience demands. And please tell the One and Two I remain grateful for their hospitality and friendship."

Alena was tapping her foot impatiently, and when Ember clambered down the bank to her, she took Ember by the hand. Ember just had enough time to cast a thin membrane around herself, before Alena gave her a hard push.

She landed face first in the water, but instead of scraping against rocks, the shallow stream had become much, much deeper, an expanse of dark blue opening out below her. Alena dived, and Ember did too. It had been a long time since she'd last been swimming. The pools in the Stones' territory were either frigid or iced over, and she avoided the sensual hot pools out of remembered embarrassment. It was wonderful being able to swim again. She was fitter now too, and she shot through the water at Alena's side, feeling like a dolphin who had unexpectedly made friends with a crocodile.

She wondered if the creatures that usually lived in the deep would impede their passage, but none did. She glimpsed some water sprites who looked as though they were about to accost them until they recognised Alena. They quickly made themselves scarce, vanishing in a thrill of bubbles.

The water quality changed as they moved from the depths of the forest into the more inhabited areas of the Swords' kingdom. It became murkier and almost thicker, but Alena didn't show any signs of being affected by it, and Ember's shield protected her from the pockets of sludge.

Finally, Alena slowed and motioned they should swim up again. They did so cautiously, eventually popping their heads up underneath a dock. The water slapped against the palings, the smell of rotting wood, waterweed, and rust in the air. Footsteps overhead made the dock shudder, and voices shouted to one another nearby.

"Riverburn," Alena whispered, and Ember nodded. Alena grasped her hand. "I'll not come closer to the pit," she said. "I cannot help you, anyway."

Ember nodded. She had suspected as much. Although the forest fae was powerful, her magic was entwined with the castle of the Swords' and didn't extend further than the castle grounds.

"The Sword will know you are here. You're too close to the heart of the kingdom for her not to sense you. Does she know what you're about?"

"Not yet," said Ember grimly. "But I don't think it will take long."

"Then run, child. Run as fast as you can." Alena took hold of Ember's hand and squeezed it. "I am a Sword and my first allegiance is to the kingdom. But Serafina is a complete brat."

Ember grinned. "Understatement." She made to swim off toward the bank, and then suddenly remembered. "By the way, the Stone mage says hello."

Alena reared back, a range of emotions flitting across her face, from pleased embarrassment to suspicion to a mask of banal ambivalence. "Does he, now? Well, if you see him again—if you live, that is—you may tell him I say hello too."

And she sank beneath the water, leaving Ember smiling to herself. She knew it. History.

Ember swam beneath the dock, unconcerned about any splashing that might give her away; the shouting of the deckhands and workers would cover any inadvertent noise she made.

One of the supporting poles had a ladder screwed to it. Once clear of the water, she shed the shield that had protected her from the depths, gratified to be dry, and cast a camouflage around herself instead. Peeking over the edge of the dock, she waited until the area was clear before climbing up and padding along the wooden boards to the wharf.

She had been here once before and all was familiar: the crowds of fae, the cries of hawkers, the cloying smells of burning charcoal, fish and waste. From the wharf, she couldn't see the pit that held the treaty, only the rising clouds of mist and smoke rising in the distance. She took the first sidestreet that pointed in the right direction and broke into a loping jog, making sure her dagger was tucked firmly into her belt.

This street was narrower and darker than the street she had strolled down with her standoffish servant Gelen. She had been a tourist then, lingering at stalls and admiring flowered courtyards. Now she was running as fast as she dared, dodging passersby, trying not to tread in the puddles of muck, not out of squeamishness, but so wet footprints wouldn't give her away. The cobbled road wound through terraced rows of houses and shops, and once through an open market with covered food stalls and crowds of fae. She slipped between pedestrians, and once, with no other option, shoved through a group, sending them stumbling backwards, confused.

The buildings and houses thinned out, and finally she glimpsed the hill that led to the temples. Each kingdom had their own temple space, and the Swords' temples were arranged around the pit that held the treaty. Mist billowed at the summit, as if it were a volcano about to erupt. As she drew closer, her confidence grew. There was no sign of guards, no sense that anyone knew she was here. She was a shadow, a wraith, a fleeting thought, a memory of movement —

Silence. Dead silence. No noise from the streets, no birdsong, no clatter of horse hooves across cobbles, no wind. Nothing, except a chilling sense of dread.

She scuttled to the side of the street, cowering against a brick wall. There was a muffled banging in her head, as though someone was playing the drums, far, far away, and she hissed between her teeth as the banging became loud and painful. She closed her eyes and to her surprise saw Ashe in front of her, as real as if her eyes were open. He was struggling to stand upright, his muscles rigid with the effort of holding himself steady. His skin was waxen and yellow, reminding her of the Adjudicator's entourage.

"Ember, they're coming." His voice was a trail of fire behind her closed lids. "I can't hold them off. You must go."

"I can't, Ashe." She spoke in a whisper, for who knew who might be listening? "Be ready."

"She found out you've been visiting me. I didn't know it was real, I thought ... She knows you're doing something ... run!"

His voice echoed through her brain, resounding against her skull, and she winced as his tone became higher, lighter. Ashe still struggled to stand before her, but he had the voice of Serafina, dripping with sweet venom. "Ember? Naughty kitty. What do you think you're doing?"

Ember didn't answer. She opened her eyes, feeling as though she might be sick. Her camouflage had disappeared, and she was too panicked to focus. Ashe was gone, but the silence of the street remained, dreadful in its stillness.

She ran.

CHAPTER 37

The houses fell away behind her, and the pavement turned into a rutted path through grass. The world dimmed as dark, threatening clouds obscured the sun and a breeze picked up, a rushing, swirling breeze that became a wind howling through the streets behind her, sending litter flying.

She took one glance back, and saw fog streaming through the streets below her, the thick white swirling fog that Ember unconsciously associated with terror and fear, because it was like that which Cole conjured.

She faced forward again, forcing her legs to pump harder, faster, as she tore up the hill. Her lungs were screaming, the blood singing in her veins, and there was a breathy whisper on the wind that sent a shaft of fear through her.

I'm coming ...

The fog streamed up the hill behind her, and Ember had a moment of clarity. Serafina was playing with her, like a cat with a mouse. She couldn't have known why Ember was there, for surely she would just appear and strike her down? No, Serafina was just taunting her, frightening her. Serafina had always been jealous of Ashe's and Cole's attraction to Ember, and a quick death wouldn't satisfy her need to prove that she was best. She wanted to hurt Ember slowly. She had no fear of a human; there was no reason for her to worry. And it was that arrogance that might just give Ember the time she needed to reach the top.

The path split into two, encircling the crater. Ember flew along the left-hand path before cutting away over patches of grass and loose gravel and heading for the summit. Flames leapt out of the pit, surrounded with choking clouds of smoke that held a curiously earthy scent of spiced tea that made her senses swim. She edged closer, glancing over her shoulder to see if the fog of Serafina's power had yet merged with the clouds of smoke and mist surrounding the temples, but it was hard to see through the eddying drifts.

A temple loomed up out of the clouds, the Temple of Swords, majestic and aloof, a little brother to the castle that she had once roamed, with turrets and columns, the symbol of crossed swords over the doorway. It faded into the mist and she refocused on her goal: the treaty that lay at the bottom of the pit.

Fae fire had never really bothered her, thanks to her innate shielding power, but this heat was intense, and she turned her head away, eyes smarting. She fumbled for the dagger at her side. All it would take was a drop of blood sprinkled on the flames. The treaty would dissolve and Ashe would be free.

For a moment, doubt pierced her and the dagger wavered in her hands. And what would happen then? She had just seen him, a shadow of who he used to be, unable to even thrust Serafina away as she used his mouth and voice to speak. What if Ashe was free but unable to prevent himself from bending to her will?

She shook her head sharply. She couldn't think like that. He had to be free to shake Serafina off completely, of that, she was sure. She gripped the dagger with a new determination and slashed the underside of her forearm. The pain was sharp and biting, and as blood welled along the line, she wiped it with her fingers, intending to flick a few drops into the crater.

"Ember." It was the voice she knew and loved. "You've hurt yourself."

"Ashe?"

Ember's voice faltered, her gaze roaming over him, greedily, as he strode out of the mist, his black cloak swirling behind him. How fine he looked! So healthy and strong, his bearing erect, colours swirling lazily beneath his skin, a rainbow of iridescence. His eyes glittered, and there was a hint of impatience in his tone.

"She's let me out to talk to you. The Sword doesn't want you to get hurt. She knows it'll hurt me if she has to hurt you, and she doesn't want that. Neither of us does. Come, Ember."

He held out his hand to her. Her first instinct was to take it, to entwine her fingers with his and let him draw her close, let him enfold her in his arms to keep her safe. But then he smiled, and an involuntary shudder went down her back. She knew that smile, the one which promised a helpless sensation of mingled hatred and desire, a feeling she associated with pleasure and pain, longing and fear.

She ignored his hand and flexed her mind. The glamour fell away from Ashe to reveal Cole, his blond hair shimmering, the achingly beautiful lines and planes of his features glowing in the mist.

"My darling." His voice held a note of surprise. "You can see me."

"Yes," she replied, a tremulous quiver in her voice. "I learned."

With two swift steps, he grasped her wrist, grinding the tender bones, forcing the dagger to fall. He twisted her arm. Her wound lay uppermost, blood smeared across her skin, and he shivered, green eyes blazing. She tried to snatch her arm away, but his grip was hurting, relentless. Slowly, he drew the torn flesh to his lips, his tongue darting out to taste. He looked up at her, blood staining his lips, his face suffused with greed and lust.

"Mine," he whispered. He dragged her to him, his arms wrapped around her, his body hard against hers, and he kissed her, forcing her mouth open, his lips hard and demanding, his tongue plundering her mouth. For a moment she wavered, wanting nothing more than to take that quick downward slide into instant lust, the sudden urge to succumb willingly as he forced her to the ground, his hands all over her body as he split her apart, and then she came back to herself, and bit down hard.

He yelped, dancing backward, his hand to his mouth, and the blood smeared across his hand wasn't just hers.

"Fuck off, Cole," she spat, and darted into the mist.

There was a roar of rage and then came Serafina's voice, shrill and enraged. "You bitch!"

Ember sprinted, her breath straining, panic welling inside her. Smoke eddied with the menacing swoop and flap of wings, drawing closer and closer. She could hear Serafina's panting; she would be upon her in seconds ...

And the Temple of Shields appeared. Previously, it had been a sketch of the real thing, an outline in a child's colouring book, but now it was complete, solid and glowing in tones of marble and amber, the sweeping roof supported by four columns, and over the door, a shield with a pine tree and three shining beads.

The front door opened.

And a hand reached out and grabbed the back of Ember's tunic, yanking her back.

Both Serafina and Cole were there, flashing back and forth in the one body, melding into one another's features so quickly, it looked as though they were glitching. Their enraged gaze flicked from Ember to the building behind her. Their eyes widened and their mouth made a little "oh" of realisation. In one quick motion, Ember closed her eyes, clenched her teeth, and head-butted them as hard as she could. They gave a screech of pain and fell back, and Ember tore up the temple stairs, the door slamming shut behind her.

CHAPTER 38

Serafina's screams cut off as the door slammed shut behind Ember. A vaulted ceiling soared overhead, and the light coming through the windows was golden and warm. The walls were carved with a lacework of beautiful patterns, edged in gold and flecked with drops of golden amber that glistened like honey. And to her surprise, the temple wasn't empty. Fae roamed around, laughing and chatting, but their joy had a vague, muted quality that reminded her of being at the border. Only this wasn't a sepia half-toned vista, but something *more* than real life. The mingled lust and terror had fallen away; the pain in her arm was a distant memory. She was at perfect peace. It would be easy to linger, to laugh and chat with these fae forever.

A female fae detached herself from the group and approached her. She was tall, with long dark hair, and her smile was welcoming and somehow familiar. Her wings were a russet colour, shot through with gold, and her eyes ...

Her eyes are like mine, Ember thought. The fae's arms came around her, holding her close, and slowly, hesitantly, Ember returned the embrace, her eyes filled with tears, a lump in her throat.

"You're my mother." Her voice broke, not with grief, but with a sense of reverence and awe, and anger too, that she had never known Wilo, her mother, in real life.

"Yes. My Amber."

Ember frowned. "They always called me Ember."

"Your father's aunt was mistaken, and you were brought forth from fire, after all."

"The car crash."

"Yes. But you were always Amber. A child of the Shields, and our last living heir."

"Do you know what I'm going to do? Will it help?"

"You will save our people. You will fulfil your destiny."

She wanted to speak, but she didn't know what to say. "I can't squash an entire lifetime into a few minutes."

"You can always return." Wilo smiled and linked her arm with Ember's. "Come."

She led Ember through the throngs of chattering fae, toward a door in the wall. It seemed like a long way away. As they walked, a thousand thoughts fluttered like butterflies through Ember's mind, but she couldn't catch any of them long enough to give them voice.

"This is my mother, and I am Amber," she murmured to herself.

She didn't much feel like an Amber though.

"I know you have questions," said Wilo, "but only a Sword can answer them."

The door swung open and Ember peeked through. There was the same warm light glowing just beyond, but instead of stillness and peace, she felt afraid. A male fae strode toward her, fast and militant, as though he was about to attack, but instead, he stopped on his side of the threshold and bowed.

Wilo curtsied, and after a bewildered moment, Ember bowed, for she still hadn't mastered a decent curtsey. The fae was handsome, with a heavy, muscular build and a beard with beaded plaits, reminding Ember of a Viking. He had a sword at his hip and he was dressed in the manner of the Swords, a military style uniform that lent itself to fighting rather than lounging.

"Do you not recognise your Blade, my lady?" he said, amusement in his voice.

Ember's mouth dropped, but she recovered quickly. "Tana. You're ... so real."

She'd only known him as a flicker in the pendant, a black shadow restlessly moving back and forth, and occasionally a zap of white-hot heat.

"The Sword is an abomination," he said simply. "The mantle of rulership in our kingdom is both a terrible burden and an unmatched honour. The Sword should be a light for the people, an inspiration of hope, not a dictator bent on squeezing the life out of all she touches. Besides, the bitch is a corpse."

"Yes," Ember agreed faintly, feeling that to do otherwise might be very unwise. To think she had held this huge, powerful fae around her neck! He gave the impression that he could barely keep his temper in check, as if one wrong word would unleash the fury of hurricanes and earthquakes.

"And to share the seat with that unworthy pup," he spat. "Even as a boy, Cole was a demon. Ashe should have won. Only his stupid sense of honour kept him from doing so."

"He felt as if he had to keep his promise to Serafina. And when she died, I suppose he felt he wasn't worthy."

"He must step up now. It's the only hope for Esha."

"They're outside." A flutter of panic began to squirm in her gut, like a restless moth trying to get out. "They're waiting for me. I have to put my blood in the pit."

She held out her arm, but to her horror, the smears had dried, the cut already congealed. She reached for her dagger to reopen the wound, but it was gone.

"A blood token will not be enough," said Tana. "Your humanity blocks it."

Ember frowned. "But Alena said ..."

"She doesn't get out much," said Tana flatly. "No doubt if you were all fae, it wouldn't be an issue."

Ember almost stamped her foot in frustration. "Then what? What must I do?"

"You must burn your human side away. Siphon your essence out. You must accept death before you may be reborn."

That word 'may' was troubling. "So it might not work, then?"

Tana gave a rueful grimace. "It might not work."

Ember's mind raced, indecision showing clearly on her face. How easy would it be to just leave, return to the Stones, beg the mage to send her to Earth and pretend none of this had ever happened? She'd done it before, and there was no Adjudicator to drag her back again.

But there was Ashe. It always came back to him.

"Then I will do as I must."

Tana nodded, and although he didn't smile, his eyes showed approval. "Do not put up your shields as you fall. The treaty must know all of you."

The moth in her stomach became a lump in her throat, and she swallowed. "Alright."

He placed a hand up to the boundary of the doorway. She copied him, their palms a whisper apart, and then he moved back into the warm light of his temple.

Her mother was still there, waiting.

"I'm going to go now," Ember said.

Wilo smiled. "Of course. But I will see you again, my dear."

Ember embraced her, and tears welled in her eyes. She could easily have stayed like this forever, warm in her mother's arms. But she broke free and crossed the temple at a run, bursting out of the doors and into the mist.

Where Serafina and Cole were waiting for her.

CHAPTER 39

Ember could see them well enough, prowling back and forth in the mist, yet they hadn't seen her. She quietly slipped down the steps. Their back was toward her, and the pit lay just ahead. But with the first crunch of her footsteps on gravel, they whipped around to glare at her, wings flicking out with a snap. They came at a run, powerful white wings beating hard, a vengeful angel of misery and death.

But Ember was fast, too. Fear gave her haste, and she tore across the path to the pit, but paused, terrified of that intense heat, of the flames. She glanced back and Serafina and Cole were there, reaching for her, mouth spread wide in a grimace of rage and triumph.

And she jumped.

A tormented cry sounded in her mind. "Ember!"

It was Ashe, his cry as broken as shattered glass, and then it faded as the flames took over.

It was like all the nightmares she'd ever had; falling into the jaws of hell, trapped in the nuclear explosion of the sun. Her instinct was to throw up a shield, but she couldn't do that, she mustn't do that. The heat took her and buffeted her, raising her and slowing her, so that she felt as if she were falling in slow motion. Her flesh was already singeing and blistering, the fabric of her clothes melting and dripping. Her skin turned black and then burst alight.

She screamed with agony, but the white heat was inside her now, scorching her vocal cords, burning her lungs away. Her blood boiled and her eyes exploded in their sockets as the flames consumed her. There was nothing between her and the fire. No shields, no barrier. She *was* fire. Her mind, her flesh, her very essence, her soul—everything that made her who she was—burned away. She was gone. She was dead. And yet ...

She hung in midair over the treaty. The simple rolled parchment lay on a stone plinth, burning as fiercely in the flames as she, and yet it was still whole. And it was curious about her. She could feel it turning her over, wondering about her, reaching into what was left of her, tasting her soul.

Fire licked her still, but the pain had burned away into nothing. She extended her hand, a skeletal shadow within dancing flames, and reached for the treaty. It was only a roll of parchment and yet it was a heavy weight, moving reluctantly from the plinth as though it didn't want to, as though it were perfectly happy to remain where it was forever. She felt it reach for her again; felt it shudder with a dawning understanding ...

The wax seal was stamped with the kingdoms' sigils: the Sands' drops of water, the wings of the Skies, the fern frond of the Seeds, the Stones' mountain peaks, and the two crossed swords of the Swords. Nothing from the Shields, of course, because they had been ground to dust—until now.

She broke the seal and a cry of pain and triumph echoed in her head, storming through her veins, and the tingle that had so often occurred between her shoulder blades turned into an agonising cramp that arched her back with a scream. The treaty crumbled in her hands, and wings burst forth from her back, heavy, huge and powerful.

Magic streamed through her, every vein, every molecule, every pore. The magic she commanded before—that strange flexing muscle—was nothing, a mere shadow of what she felt now. Her mind expanded to encompass the whole of Esha, of the galaxy in which the world hung, and then shrank to a pinpoint as she gazed at the pile of ash in her hands, the atoms of it, its subatomic particles, watched them disappear. The treaty was gone, and so was the old Ember. Both gone forever.

She looked up to the sliver of sky just visible through the flames, and her wings obeyed, pumping hard as she shot up and up, like molten rock spewing from a volcano, borne on the back of a golden flame as she erupted into the world.

Far below, Serafina writhed on the edge of the pit. Like a cicada splitting its skin, her brother crawled out of her, hands gripping at clods of earth and tufts of grass as he sought to tear himself free. Serafina screamed, her hands clawing at her scalp as though her mind were causing her untold agonies. As Ember's shadow fell across them, both looked up, eyes wide, realisation hitting both of them as they beheld her true self.

Serafina gave one last high-pitched scream, and then she simply blew apart, her dead self finally coming to terms with the fact that she was gone. The dust of her whirled in the breeze, scattering wide and settling as though she had never been.

Ember gently lowered herself to touch ground, and Cole scrambled back. Slowly, he got to his feet, with some semblance of his old cockiness back.

"Ember. You look different."

"Hush," she said, and her voice was different too. Stronger. Wilder. She could feel the power in it as it folded itself around Cole and squeezed tight, making him hiss like an angry cat.

With effort, he said, "Stop that."

He lashed out with his own enchantment, a sword designed to flay the very skin from her flesh. But she had learned. And unlike Cole, she had never underestimated her opponent. She already had a shield up and his killing blow was the mere stroke of a careless finger.

"You're going to die now," she told him, and his features blanched white, his beauty drained, his face like a bleached skull.

"You cannot kill me!" He was frantic, almost gibbering, and she could feel his sword striking at her, again and again, desperate to find a way in. "I am the Sword now. And you are nothing."

"I am the Shield protecting my people." She snapped her wings, creating a gust of wind that made him stagger back. "I am the last Shield. Do you know how powerful that makes me? Everything in that land is now in me."

"There is nothing in that land! It was obliterated! We razed it to the ground!"

"You should have killed all of us. That was your ancestors' mistake. We didn't die. Not all of us. We lived."

She crooked a finger, and Cole roared with anger as his feet left the ground. With the force of her will, she could carry him, she could bend him.

She could break him.

"*I* didn't do it. It wasn't me. You can't blame me for what my ancestors did."

"You benefit from what your ancestors did. You used that stolen magic. And you were about to do it to the Seeds, and the Sands, and everyone else."

"But I didn't! You're judging me for things I haven't done. I am the Sword! And you owe me a little fucking respect!"

"I owe you nothing."

And she raised her hands and threw him into the pit.

CHAPTER 40

She sank to the ground, her wings folding around her as if to protect her from the world. She felt drained, exhausted. All she wanted to do was cry. Serafina was gone. Cole was gone. And Ashe …

She closed her eyes, felt hot tears well under her lids. She had stripped herself down to fae for him. Had torn apart his kingdom and likely caused havoc on Earth too. And who would be her ally? A ruler of dirt and rocks and the hint of a stream trickling through the wasteland, queen of a people in hiding for generations?

All for him. And with Serafina and Cole gone, he was gone too, and she was alone.

She lifted her head and gazed at the pit in misery, the flames still merrily leaping high as though nothing had happened, when in fact, everything had happened. A flash of light flew out of the pit, and she drew back as it landed with a *clink* in front of her.

She gazed at the orange jewelled pendant hanging on a heavy chain in disbelief and reached out a tremulous hand to touch it. With a thunderous crack, the gem shattered.

A wisp of black smoke rose from the shards, a wisp that grew thick and choking, and then the black smoke cleared away to reveal a figure sprawled on the ground, pale and unmoving.

"Ashe!" She scrambled over to him, her hand to his face. His skin was cold, his features lax. Fighting a growing unease, she shook him. "Ashe?"

But he remained still.

Frantically, she shook him again and pressed two fingers to his neck for a pulse.

Nothing.

She called him again and again, but there was no response, and eventually she fell still, sucking in a shuddering breath and finally allowing the tears to fall. She tipped back her head and howled, howled her grief and rage at the world that had given her life and taken his. There was nothing left for her now, and she collapsed against his chest sobbing, her wings stretching out to cover him, to shield him.

And then ...

A tremor. She thought her longing was playing tricks on her. But there it was again. Beneath her cheek, she felt it, heard it. A heartbeat. Hardly daring to believe it, she sat back. Had she imagined that flush in his cheeks, the slow swirl of colours beneath his skin? She chafed his hands, trying to bring some warmth back to them, and called his name again. "Ashe, my darling. Wake up. It's time to wake up."

He groaned, his eyelids fluttering open, his eyes at first unfocused, and suddenly blazing and alert.

"Ember?"

He struggled to sit, and then she was crying and laughing, tears streaming down her face as she hugged him tight. "You're alive. And they're dead. They're gone, and you're free."

"And you ..." his face was a moon of confusion. "You have wings."

"Yes," she told him. "Bit of a story there."

She helped him to his feet. Although his strength was returning quickly, he couldn't seem to let go of her hand, couldn't take his eyes from her.

"You're fae."

"I'm a Shield. The only heir."

He gently stroked her wing, and she shivered. She had felt it as a hand caressing her bare skin and he smiled, slyly, before his attention shifted to the pit.

"I should be angry that the Sword was defeated. I should be furious that the Sword was defeated by a *Shield*. And yet ... I'm just relieved. Their rulership was cursed. It should never have been. Serafina was always troubled. I should never have promised to take her place as the Blade if I won. I was just ..."

"You were in love." Ember nodded, and a fleeting image of an angry human face shouting at her as she cowered in a corner slipped into her mind before it vanished. "We put up with terrible things when we're in love. We do stupid things. Cole only won because of your guilt. You were always stronger than him. You let him win that last contest."

"And I would have won the tournament if it weren't for you," he told her with a dose of heavy sarcasm, and she laughed.

"I apologise. But you're the ruler now. It was always your destiny. And you won't need a trapped Blade to help you. You can find someone to sit at your side. Like Sten and Ruby."

He looked at her, his gaze serious. "And what of you?"

She flexed her wings, and the feathers rippled in alternating shades of golden honey. She didn't think she'd ever tire of that.

"I shall go to my new home. Rebuild. My mother will help me. All my ancestors will. And the fae who left will return. We will be stronger for our absence."

He looked askance at that, and she asked, somewhat indignantly, "Do you not believe me?"

He raised a gentle hand and stroked her face. "I hoped you might come back to the Swords with me. I don't think I can bear to let you go."

He leaned in, and she let her eyes drift closed. But he didn't kiss her, and she opened her eyes again. He was frowning. "What now?"

"You smell different," he informed her. "Not as spicy."

Her mouth dropped in shock, and she leaned into his neck and inhaled before pulling back. "You smell different, too."

They gazed at each other in mingled bewilderment and regret and then broke into twin gasps of laughter. He pulled her to him and kissed her properly and she clung to him, feeling the heat of his body coalesce with hers. Her desire was mounting quickly, as though the fire of the pit was burning through every molecule of her, and she ached to have him again, and again.

She pulled away, her eyes blazing. "You always said that fae can break humans. What can fae do to fae?"

He gathered her up in his arms, and his black wings erupted from his back. He lifted her into the air and nuzzled her neck, murmuring. "Would you like to find out?"

She smiled, a provocative smile of anticipation and desire. "Oh, yes."

CHAPTER 41

A mber sat on the throne, the tawny-gold beads in her crown reflecting the light as she scanned the room. The guards were in full gleaming uniform, erect and motionless, the servants waiting, perfectly composed, the courtiers dressed to elegant perfection and murmuring softly to one another. Music filled the air, the lilting tones doing nothing to soothe her nerves. Glin leaned toward her, features composed. "Be still. All is well."

"'Well' isn't good enough. It has to be perfect." In the past year since Amber had assumed rulership, Glin had become like an older sister to her, and she was an easy choice to make as her ruling counterpart while her people slowly trickled back to their lands.

Radi oscillated between being overjoyed at being a princess of the court with all the comforts that came along with it, and chafing under the close eye of her new tutors who were determined to teach her a raft of new things, from reading and writing to dancing and deportment. Often, she went missing, only to be found helping the servants in the kitchens, or digging in the gardens. It was difficult for her to settle into her new role, although her mother came to it as if she were born to it.

Willing hands and a great deal of magic had rebuilt the palace of Shields. The Stone mage had gifted enchantments of stone-working and building, and, not to be outdone, Alena had donated her knowledge too. The rest came from the other rulers of the kingdoms—bar the Skies, of course, who had merely sent their best wishes. Amber had restored it to her mother's memory of it as a child, a graceful building with long avenues of conifers, and it combined the best of what Amber had loved at the Swords' castle, as well as the Stones' palace.

She struggled to imagine new things now. The Stone mage and Alena had sent her the pictures she'd painted in their kingdoms, and she'd hung them everywhere. They were like talismans, reminders of who she used to be. She lingered in front of them often, wondering how she had ever created them. It was as though someone else had made them, someone she'd once known long, long ago. And although it sometimes made her sad to see what she had lost, her overwhelming feeling was of pride and satisfaction that she'd once been able to do that at all. Ember was an artist and a dreamer. Amber was a queen.

Swirl sent a host of centaurs to build the healing clinics and schools they were renowned for, and the Seeds had filled the clinic shelves with precious medicines and potions distilled from rare jungle plants, for they were only too happy not to be caught up in a war not of their making. Of course, they still eyed the grasslands with a covetous air, but hopefully, it would be a long while before they attempted to do anything about it.

Sten and Ruby hadn't visited yet. They had been generous in their gifts, but she wasn't entirely sure if that came from affection or politics. They had declined to visit, and Amber suspected the rumour that

Apoli hadn't yet returned home might have had something to do with it.

The land itself was blooming with fresh life, a perpetual spring bower, as though rejoicing after a long, hard winter. Every morning, the ruined earth retreated further, to be replaced by a carpet of green grass and wildflowers. Glin often reminded her that its new life was because of her, and despite Amber's protestations, her people agreed. They were fierce in their loyalty, they who had suffered so much, and were now free to live and love in the lands of their ancestors. Settlements were growing and would soon become villages and towns, and the creeping beasts who roamed the empty wasteland in the faes' absence were being pushed further and further out to the granite mountains.

But this was the first proper diplomatic envoy Amber had ever hosted, and she was anxious. Everything that happened would be reported back to the other rulers. She knew they were scandalised that a once-human had not only defeated the ruling Sword, but had restored the Shields to its place in Esha. She suspected that all were waiting for her to make some terrible mistake so they could swoop in and scoop up her burgeoning kingdom.

A tap on her arm interrupted her reverie, and her advisor leaned close and whispered, "Our guests are just outside, Your Majesty."

Amber shot to her feet, and Glin tugged her back down again.

"Sit," she said firmly. "You're the ruler, not a servant."

"Nor am I a dog," Amber hissed, amused. "Don't tell me to sit!"

Glin covered her mouth with her hands, and both tried to control their giggles. The advisor gave them a stern look, and when the two had composed themselves, Amber signalled the guards to open the doors.

In they marched, a host of guards in a familiar silver armour, and then as they peeled off to the left and right in formation, the Sword entered and her heart swelled. A gathering of courtiers and advisors came with him, and all stood silently as Ashe strode to the centre of the room and bowed. "Your Majesty."

She bobbed her head, eyes dancing. "Your Majesty."

He straightened and gave her a smile, an intimate smile that warmed her to her toes. She couldn't prevent her gaze from going over him hungrily, taking in the broad shoulders, dark eyes that crackled with energy, the lean muscle of his arms and legs. She hadn't seen him in months, and the anticipation of his visit had kept her in a fever of impatience. She bit her lip, thinking of the last time she'd seen him, when he'd shown her exactly what fae can do to fae, and his eyes were immediately drawn to her mouth. When their eyes met again, it was as though there was no one else in the room, and she could feel that familiar stirring in her gut, her muscles becoming languid, as a wet heat blossomed.

Her advisor eventually gave an irritated cough, and she was brought back to her senses, saying hurriedly, "Welcome to the Kingdom of Shields. The Kingdom of Swords is very welcome at our court. This is our queen, Glin."

Glin gave a gracious nod, and Ashe bowed to her, and said, "You Majesties, may I present my co-regent—"

"Co-regent?" Amber said, surprised, and the advisor gave another cough, louder this time. "Sorry. I thought you were going to call him your Blade."

"We've done away with all that. No Sword. No Blade. We are rulers together."

A male fae stepped forward, smiling bashfully, his wings like stained glass. "Hello Ember. I mean, Amber. I mean, Your Majesty."

"Tasar!" And this time, she did get up, despite her advisor's coughing fit, moving swiftly down the dais stairs, and embracing him warmly. This fae had taught her to see through glamours and to paint her own; the brother of a maid, who had been murdered by the heir, was now a king. It was as though a circle was becoming complete.

"There were too many at court divided between Cole, Serafina and me," Ashe explained. "Too many factions, too many quarrels. So I asked Alena for advice, and she was only too happy to provide it. He has proved to be a fine choice."

"Congratulations!" she said to Tasar, but she was finding it hard to keep her gaze from Ashe. She wanted to drink in his features, linger on his smile. His hand brushing hers felt like an electric shock going up her arm, and she couldn't help a sigh of utter longing. His eyes darkened, a muscle twitched in his jaw, and his hand jerked as if preventing himself from yanking her to him.

"I think we should make all our visitors welcome," came Glin's amused voice. The music swelled, servants offered refreshments and wine, and the courtiers mingled with the visitors, offering toasts and sharing news, some already beginning to dance.

"You'll have to forgive us," Amber said over the chatter and laughter. "Our court is new and unseasoned and I'm afraid formality isn't something we're very good at yet."

"Oh dear," Ashe said, with mock severity. "You may be fae, but I'm afraid you will never act like it. I wonder how long the diplomacy between our kingdoms will last?"

She stepped closer, feeling the heat rise between them. "I should think diplomatic relations between the Swords and the Shields will be very sweet indeed," she murmured with an arch smile, and he laughed, sweeping her into his arms.

THE END

And Finally …

Thank you for reading the third story set in the fairytale world of Esha! If you enjoyed it, please consider giving it a rating or review on your favourite book platform. For more info on all things Esha, visit https://www.tabithaday.com/

Discover a new adventure set in the Kingdom of Skies
Chronicles of Esha 4